Simon & Schuster Books for Young Readers

JUDITH LOGAN LEHNE

COYOTE GIRL

SIMON & SCHUSTER BOOKS FOR YOUNG READERS
An imprint of Simon & Schuster Children's Publishing Division
1230 Avenue of the Americas
New York, New York 10020
Text copyright © 1995 by Judith Logan Lehne
Frontispiece copyright © 1995 by Leslie Bowman
SIMON & SCHUSTER BOOKS FOR YOUNG READERS
is a trademark of
Simon & Schuster.
Designed by Anahid Hamparian
The text of this book is set in 13-point Dutch 766.
Manufactured in the United States of America
10 9 8 7 6 5 4 3 2 1
Library of Congress Cataloging-in-Publication Data

Lehne, Judith Logan.
Coyote Girl / by Judith Logan Lehne
p.   cm.
Summary: Running away after the random stabbing of her mother, a junior
high school girl encounters a wounded coyote pup and nurses him in an
abandoned root cellar in the Wisconsin woods.
[1. Mothers and daughters—Fiction.   2. Death—Fiction.
3. Grief—Fiction.   4. Runaways—Fiction.   5. Coyotes—Fiction.
6. Wisconsin—Fiction.]   I. Title.
PZ7.L53253Co   1995   [Fic]—dc20   94-38683 CIP   AC
ISBN: 0-689-80287-0

To Todd & Tessa

research assistants, indefatigable readers,
merciless critics, and devoted supporters.
T. G. I. L. Y.

ACKNOWLEDGMENTS

Writing is a solitary experience, but only through a writer's interactions with real, breathing humans can a fictional story blossom from the heart and mind into believable printed words. With thanks to Jackie DeBauche, Director of Rehabilitation at the Northwoods Wildlife Center in Minocqua, Wisconsin, for generously sharing her knowledge of coyotes so that I could bring them to life in this story.

Thanks also to Kendra, Ed, Shane, Kyle, Patty, Karen, Rich, and Reup; each of you had an important part in this work. And a prayer of thanks for the miracle that sent David Gale, patient, considerate, and expert editor, into my professional life.

ONE

As soon as Ma brought the package from under the Christmas tree, Billie knew her wish hadn't come true. But then, she'd never really expected it to. She forced a smile as she held the lumpy gift. Ma fluttered about on tiptoes, hardly able to contain herself. Billie couldn't imagine what would bring such sparkle to Ma's eyes.

The wrappings fell away, and Billie was speechless. She hadn't known what to anticipate inside the shiny red paper; perhaps an electric alarm clock, so she wouldn't have to awaken anymore to the ear-splitting clatter of her wind-up one. But she'd never have figured on *this* gift.

She held the round, plastic music box in the palm of her hand and stared at the figurines in ballroom dress on top. The lady's blonde hair was peeling in places, looking strangely like Ma's when she waited too long to bleach the roots. Only one black dot clung to the place where the man's eyes should be, and the lone eye stared blankly across the room. Billie looked where the eye pointed, at Roger rubbing a shaky hand across his unshaven face. Billie wondered if Roger could see any better than the plastic, one-eyed man.

"Here," Ma said, taking the music box from Billie's loose grasp. "Wind it. The music's beautiful, Billie—like merry-go-rounds and . . ." Her eyes grew glazed, faraway, and Billie knew Ma was going back to the carnival ride they'd taken last summer.

Billie glanced back at Roger. He peered out the window at the falling snow, scratching his stomach and mumbling.

Ma turned the bottom knob while holding the figurines on top; the *click-clicking* noise echoed in the silence. Only after she'd set the box down on the table did Ma let go of the dancing couple. Immediately, they turned on their gold-painted pedestal as tinny music played. Ma spun too, twirling her arms in the air, then bringing them down so it looked like she was waltzing with an invisible man.

"There's a magical someplace," she sang, ". . . with songs to sing . . ." Her voice was raspy from too many cigarettes, but she didn't seem to notice. "Though snow drifts are hiding the promise of spring . . ."

Billie folded her arms across her chest. A music box. It wasn't the kitten she'd hoped for, but the music brought joy into the room, and gaiety to Ma's face. Maybe a different wish would be answered.

Ma continued to dance around the room with her imaginary partner, dipping gracefully as they passed the little tree with its one string of lights. Her reflection shimmered and blurred in the silver ornament from Ma's childhood. Year round, the silver ball hung from a string in the kitchen window of whatever place was their home, and Billie had watched it grow tarnished and chipped with time. But at Christmas, Ma always found a tree of some sort and gave the silver ball a place of honor on the nicest branch. Billie never saw the chips and tarnishes on it then; it always sparkled like a globed mirror.

The music wound down, and Ma's dancing and singing slowed, too. ". . . some—place—with—songs. . . ."

Even with her uncombed hair and dingy bathrobe, Ma was beautiful when she danced and sang. And laughed. Billie had nearly forgotten how really lovely Ma could be, especially when she was daydreaming. And that's what she's doing now, Billie thought: dreaming of castles and satin gowns and a prince. Billie picked up the music box to rewind it. Ma's dreaming could be contagious, and Billie wanted all of them to catch it today.

"Kee-rist!" Roger said, suddenly leaping from the hassock. "That ~~tinkle~~ *tinkle-tinkle* noise is giving me a headache." He grabbed Ma by the arm and she spun to a stop just like the chipped-hair lady on the pedestal. "You act like a fool," he said. Her eyes stopped sparkling, and the smile slid off her face.

So much for your dreams, Ma, Billie thought. She picked up the Christmas wrappings and watched Roger stomp into the kitchen. His undershirt flapped around the sagging seat of his gray sweats. And so much for Prince Charming, too.

Billie carried the music box into her room and set it on her dresser. "Songs to sing," she said, scowling at the plastic dancers. How could Ma keep dreaming her fairy tales, when they never came true? Billie remembered the wonderful fantasy Ma had spun for herself and Billie, when Roger came into their lives three years ago.

The night Billie met Roger, Ma had told her, "He's handsome—and he has a steady job." She was singing as she blew dust off the coffee table and straightened the flowered sheet that hid the worn sofa fabric. "He could be a good daddy for you."

So Billie took special care to comb her hair in a neat part, like Ma liked it, then set to drawing a picture for Ma's new friend. She drew a man in yellow coveralls lying underneath a jungle-green car. Ma said Roger was going to have his own car repair shop someday, so Billie printed ROGER'S AUTO SERVICE across the top of the page in huge purple letters. But when Roger came to the apartment, he didn't take the paper Billie held out to him. He just looked at Ma and said, "A kid, huh?" and went into the kitchen so Ma could fix him a drink. And even though Billie had only been nine, she'd known that Ma's Roger-dreams probably weren't any different from all the others she'd been painting onto Billie's heart for as long as Billie could remember.

Sometimes Billie lay in bed at night, listening to murmurings from Ma and Roger's room. Ma, going on and on about Roger quitting his job at the station and buying his own shop—and Roger hollering "Wishin' don't make money grow on trees, Carolyn!" Billie suspected that once, Roger had gotten caught in some of Ma's dreams, but now he only shook his head and swore when she tried to spin him into her magical thinking.

There were times when Billie herself thought about telling Ma, "Grow up. Your dreams are too big to ever come true." But other times, like only minutes ago when Billie had let the music trill wishes across the back of her mind, she wanted to know how to make fairy tales in her head, like Ma did. She wanted Ma to tell *her* how to grow *down*. It was hard, sometimes, to keep fantasies alive.

Billie heard pans rattling on the stove, and Ma speaking low. Roger's voice boomed above the cooking sounds. "Christmas is just another day, Carolyn. A day off with pay, is all. You act like you're waitin' for Santa Claus to arrive."

At the mention of Santa, Billie knew that, yes, there were still times she let herself get caught up in hoping. Like last month when she and Ma were walking home from the store and saw the lady on the corner with the cardboard box. Ma had tried to pull her away, but Billie saw the word KITTENS scrawled across the front of the box. She only wanted to take a quick peek.

"Nine weeks old yesterday," the lady said, pulling her scarf tight under her chin. Snow fluffed around the box as Billie lifted the flap. Six striped kittens squirmed together in one corner, mewing loudly.

"Ma, come look," Billie said. "They're so adorable."

Ma raised an eyebrow and let a puff of air out of her mouth in a rush, but she did come to look in the box.

"Three dollars each," the lady said. "Make a sweet Christmas gift."

That's when Billie saw the little gray dustball huddled alone in the corner opposite the others. He made no sounds, but stared right up at Billie with eyes of robin's-egg blue. She bent to touch his fur, and the kitten snuggled around her hand. "Why's this one all by itself?" she asked. Ma began to tap her foot on the sidewalk.

"It's the runt. The mother didn't want nothin' to do with it, and neither do the other babies." The lady grabbed one of the striped kittens by the scruff of its neck and held it up to Billie. "That gray one's peculiar," she said. "But this one'd be a darlin' Christmas pet."

"My husband doesn't like animals," Ma said. "C'mon, Billie. He'll be wanting dinner soon."

All the way home, Billie begged. "I'll keep him in my room . . . I'll get a job to pay for his food . . . Roger won't even know he's there." The gray kitten's eyes, the feel of his soft purring under her hand made her push at Ma harder than she'd ever before dared. Every day for a week she went to see the lady on the corner, then reported to Ma as, one-by-one, the striped kittens found homes. When the gray one was left alone in the box and the lady told Billie, "If no one buys it by tomorrow, I'm takin' it to the pound," Billie finally caught Ma up in her dream.

"But the lady said he was sickly," Ma said.

"No, she said 'peculiar.' But I've watched him every day, Ma. He's just different from the rest. Quieter. Roger would like a *quiet* pet."

"He was a little cutie, wasn't he?" Ma sat at the kitchen table and smiled. "I had a kitten once, did I tell you? His name was Butterscotch. He was tan with white paws and—" She frowned, and her mouth stretched tight. "My mother . . . got rid of him." When she turned to Billie, her eyes were watery. "I'll talk to Roger, but don't expect miracles."

"I won't," Billie replied.

But as the scent of bacon made its way into her bedroom now, Billie realized that she *had* expected a miracle.

Roger was already eating when Billie went into the kitchen, his head close to his plate as he shoveled eggs and bacon into his mouth. Ma was by the stove, buttering toast. She raised her eyebrows to Billie and cocked her head in Roger's direction. Billie nodded, and pulled the metal chair from her place at the table, careful not to let it clank across the linoleum. When Ma set down Billie's breakfast, Roger lifted his eyes briefly, and scowled.

Billie concentrated on her eggs, chewing each forkful exactly eight times. She listened to the sound her teeth and tongue made before she swallowed, and watched Ma push food around her plate without eating anything. She wondered if Ma was remembering the last Christmas she and Billie had shared before Roger came into their world. Billie remembered.

The Christmas tree was only as tall as a yardstick, and there were no electric lights that year. But Santa still came, bringing Billie a box of paper dolls, and Ma smiled when she put on the star necklace Billie had made for her at school. For breakfast, Ma made tree-shaped green pancakes.

"Can't afford lights for the little pine," she said to Billie as she slathered butter on the pancakes, "but that doesn't mean we can't sparkle up these trees!" Ma and Billie laughed as they sprinkled mounds of red sugar on the steaming pancake trees.

That had been the Michigan Christmas, just

before they moved to Minnesota and Ma met Roger. Ma had been full of laughter those months when Roger came calling. Billie remembered how Roger would bust through the door on Friday nights, bringing gifts for Ma every time: flower bouquets from the grocery store, a whole bag of Ma's favorite candy bars, once even a dress from a store Ma said was too fancy for most folks to go into. Sometimes Roger brought Billie presents, too: comic books and rainbow-colored suckers. By the time Ma and Roger were married, Billie had begun to believe, like Ma, that Roger really was the answer to their dreams. Billie didn't know exactly when the dreams started to fall apart, but there were barely any traces left that Billie could recognize. Minnesota Christmases had electric tree lights, but never any green pancake trees or red sugar sprinkles.

Billie jumped when Roger's chair clattered away from the table. He slapped a booklet of McDonald's coupons in front of her plate.

"Here, kid, M'rry Chris'ms," he mumbled as he left the kitchen.

Ma's eyes smiled at Billie. She leaned close and whispered, "Now, wasn't that sweet of him?"

Billie shrugged and began to clear the table. As she filled the sink with hot water and watched the soap churn into airy white snow hills, she thought about the words of the music box song. *Though snow drifts are hiding the promise of spring* . . .

When the dishes were draining, Billie ran her cupped hand through the soap-snow, shoving the remaining bubbles to one side, and stared at the murky dishwater. No, she thought. There won't be "songs to sing." Not even when the snow is gone. Not here.

TWO

The clanging of her alarm clock brought Billie from sleep as abruptly as if someone had shaken her. She fumbled around for the off button, then rolled back over, pulling the blankets tight to her chin. She waited for Ma to come in and warn her, "If you don't get out of bed this minute, you're gonna be walking to school." While she waited, she tried to recapture the dream she'd been having before the alarm ripped it apart, but the pictures wouldn't come back.

In the darkness of the January morning, she could hear icy pellets spitting against her window, but she couldn't hear Ma clinking cereal bowls and slamming cupboard doors. She sat up and listened harder. The refrigerator was whining, like always, and water bubbled up in the radiator behind the sofa.

Billie moved slowly through the apartment, pulling the quilt Ma made last winter around her shoulders. The bathroom door across from her bedroom was open, but Ma wasn't at the sink penciling on her eyebrows or brushing color onto her cheeks. Billie looked across the hall at the closed door to the other bedroom, then checked the living room and the kitchen. Both rooms were exactly as she'd left them last night, when she gave up waiting for Ma and Roger to come home. Even the stove light was still on.

Billie hesitated before knocking on Ma's and Roger's door. After two loud raps, she eased the door open and glanced around the room. The blankets on Ma's side of the bed were still tucked in, but Roger's side was tangled and tossed back, and his pillow was on the floor. Hadn't Ma come home last night, or had she been home and left earlier? And where was Roger now? Billie wondered as she dressed quickly and made her lunch.

She wasn't aware of how rapidly her heart had been pounding until she heard footsteps coming up the outside stairs. She slapped bologna between two slices of bread and peered out the kitchen door.

"What're you gawkin' at?" Roger said, pushing past her. His boots made dirty puddles on the floor as he tromped across the room to set a carton of milk on the counter.

Billie looked down the steps. She shivered and closed the door. "Where's Ma?" she asked.

Roger threw his coat on Ma's chair. "Beats ~~the hell outta~~ me," he said. There were dark circles under his eyes, and his hands trembled as he pulled a cigarette from his shirt pocket.

Billie shoved her sandwich into a bag. "You were with her last night, Roger. Where is she?"

Roger tapped cigarette ashes into a saucer and ran his fingers through his hair.

"Roger!" Billie shouted, standing in front of him. "Did she come home last night at *all*?"

Roger stubbed out the cigarette and jumped to his feet. He glared down at Billie. "Don't talk t'me like that!" Smoke puffed into Billie's face. "This ain't any of your business."

Billie bit back the words she wanted to shout at Roger, and took a deep breath. "You've got to go to work," she said, coating each word with counterfeit sweetness. "I'll wait here for—"

"She knows what time school starts," Roger said. "And she knows when I leave for work. If she wanted t'be here, she'd be here now." He went into his bedroom and returned with his grease-stained Mobil Service coveralls. "Now get goin'!"

Billie slumped in her seat as the bus crept along the icy back roads to the rural stops, then turned onto the main road through Compton toward the junior high. The sound of the big tires swooshing through the salt-melted ice drowned out most of the chatter around her, but Billie could hear Jenna Milhoney's voice screeching across the aisle, bragging about her Christmas haul.

"Awesome, huh?" Angie Dijackimo said, elbowing Billie. "I got new jeans, too—" She lifted her hips off the seat and pulled her parka up to her waist. "See? But they're not the designer kind like Jenna's."

Billie smiled at Angie. "They're still nice."

"What'd you get for Christmas?" Angie asked, settling back onto the seat cushion.

"Some stuff . . . a music box," Billie answered.

"Is it porcelain? I collect porcelain music boxes," Angie said, then went on to describe each one.

Billie half-listened, nodding when she thought it might be the polite thing to do, but her mind was back at the apartment. Where had Ma gone last night? And why wasn't she home now? If she'd had to open up Dolly's Kitchen this morning to help Dolly get ready for the breakfast crowd, she'd have told Billie last night.

"Bil-lie!" Angie's voice whined. "Are you coming, or not?"

Billie hadn't felt the bus stop. She hoisted her

duffle bag over her shoulder and followed Angie into school. Angie stopped in front of Billie's locker. "I'd love to see your music box. Maybe after school sometime, huh?"

"Yeah, maybe," Billie said, as Angie continued down the hall.

It was always hard for Billie to concentrate in class on the first day back after a vacation, but it was doubly difficult today. Her mind kept wandering back to last night, before Ma and Roger left. Ma, dressed in jeans and a western shirt, spent a long time teasing her hair so it pouffed away from her face. That probably meant she and Roger had gone some place where there was country music. She remembered the truck back-firing a couple of times before it rumbled out to the street. If they'd been going to Stuffy's Tap down the block, they'd have walked. If they'd been at The Northwestern in Edgar, Roger might have wanted to go home before Ma was ready to quit dancing. That had happened once in October. But then Roger got a ride home, and Ma kept the truck. Roger had the truck this morning. Why didn't he know where Ma was? Maybe he did know, but he wasn't telling. . . .

All through the day, the questions swirled in her head, meddling with her concentration even as her pencil moved across her papers. Now as Miss Haynes rambled on with instructions for a group Social Studies project, Billie hoped she'd at least written down the homework assignments correctly; she didn't need any teachers hassling her tomorrow.

"We'll divide up into small groups," Miss Haynes said. She moved among the rows, tapping each desk. "One, two, three, four, five, six: you're Group A; one, two . . ."

Billie tried to figure out which group she'd be in.

Miss Haynes tapped Ty Smythe's desk, in front of Billie's. "Six! You're the last group," she said. Her eyebrows raised up as she noticed Billie. It had been four months since Billie had come to Compton Junior High, but Miss Haynes seemed to forget about the extra desk almost as often as she forgot where she'd left her pink chalk.

"Oh, dear. Well!" She scanned the class. "I suppose Group E will have one extra member!" She tapped Billie's desk and waddled back to the front of the room.

Ty tossed a disgusted look over his shoulder. "Great. The boy-girl," he muttered.

Billie glared at Ty's back, and tried to fluff up her hair. How was it, she wondered, that Ma could spend years dreaming of fairy tale princesses, and still make Billie keep her hair clipped so close to her head?

"Long hair's too much of a bother," Ma would say, even when Billie got old enough to take care of it herself. If Billie argued, Ma moved the shears more rapidly, making an even-deeper pile of brown clippings on the floor.

Perhaps that was it, Billie thought as Miss Haynes droned on at the blackboard; princesses have silky *blonde* hair, not grocery-sack-brown. At the sound of rustling pages, Billie opened her Social Studies book. Short hair, and a boy's name; the combination had been trouble since kindergarten. She guessed Ma thought the name was a gift, but that was just another one of Ma's bungled plans. She thought now of all the times she'd heard the story: How Carolyn Rowe had fallen in love with a "blue-eyed man in a red sedan"—a man named Billy. In Ma's drawl, the words sounded like corny song lyrics. In fact, the whole story, if set to music, could have made the Top Ten Country charts. Billie could just imagine Patty Loveless singing sorrowfully about the girl who waited for the blue-eyed man, waited even after the baby was born, but the guy never returned. The chorus would go something like:

"'I'll marry you, I'll marry you, when I come back to town,' said the blue-eyed man in the red sedan, but he let poor Carolyn down."

Ma said he vanished into thin air; just up and disappeared, like he'd been nothing more than one of her dreams. She never said if Billie was part of the dream.

Miss Haynes pointed to the outline on the blackboard. "Bring your ideas to your group tomorrow, and—" Blessedly, the dismissal bell cut her off.

Billie rushed to the bus and plunked down in the first seat, behind the driver, sure that no one would sit next to her in that spot, not even Angie.

By the time Angie scrambled up the bus steps, most of the seats were taken. She raised her eyebrows when she saw Billie.

"C'mon to the back," she said. "We'll find some place to squeeze in together."

"That's okay," Billie said. "I don't want to move all my junk."

Poor Angie, Billie thought as she watched her settle for a seat next to Suzanne Bartishofski. Suzanne would delight in harassing Angie for the entire ride. But Billie knew Angie would stare straight ahead without saying a word; Angie knew how to handle herself, that was clear. Since moving to Compton, Billie'd thought that if she ever had a friend, she'd like one like Angie.

Angie gave a little shrug and sent Billie a sideways smile. Maybe, Billie thought, I *could* let Angie come over sometime. Maybe—once I find out how long we're staying. It didn't pay to make friends too quickly; it just made the leaving harder.

The bus driver down-shifted and the bus wheezed to a stop. Billie hurried along the sidewalk. Surely Ma was home by now. The sky was darkening, and the air had the bitter-damp feel of coming snow. Billie pulled her coat collar up over her mouth and nose as she turned toward the faded-pink house that had been converted into two apartments. She wished Ma had gotten the first-floor apartment with the rickety, but gigantic, front porch; it was perfect for year-round roller skating. Billie sighed. Old man Richter kept the porch cluttered with busted-up furniture and bags of old newspapers. What a waste of space.

The steps to Billie's apartment climbed up the side of the house, past Mr. Richter's bedroom window, to the landing in front of the upstairs kitchen door. Mr. Richter was spying from behind the curtain when Billie passed by.

"Hi, Mr. Busybody!" she said. The curtain

immediately fell back across the window.

Weird, Billie thought. He usually spies only at night.

A policeman came out of the kitchen just as Billie reached the landing. He looked strangely at her, then faced Roger. "You'll need to come down to the station," he said.

"Yeah, sure," Roger replied.

"I'm sorry," the officer said, adjusting his hat. His shiny black shoes clattered down the steps.

Billie dropped her duffle bag on the floor and pulled off her hat and gloves. Roger stood frozen-still in the middle of the kitchen. His head bobbed as if it were attached to his shoulders by a weak spring. A cigarette burned in the saucer on the table, but Roger pulled another from his pocket and lit it. His eyes looked glazed, like those of a blind person—and wet; wet with tears. Ma wasn't home. A knot formed in Billie's stomach.

"The police—Ma—Roger, what's going on?" Billie stammered.

Roger sat at the table and buried his face in his hands. His voice was muffled. Billie had to sit right beside him to hear his words. "Mugged," he said. "Her throat—she was knifed."

The room began to spin in front of Billie's eyes. "Ma?"

Roger shook his head from side to side. The snuffling sounds coming from behind his hands sent shivers down Billie's arms. She put her hand on his shoulder. "Roger?" She squeezed gently. "Who, Roger? Who was—"

Roger raised his head slowly and stared straight at Billie. "Your ma, kid." His voice was softer than Billie had ever heard it.

She could feel the blood surging hot through her veins, until it seemed to pool inside her head, thumping, thumping, thumping in her ears. Behind her eyes, she saw Ma's smiling face as she bent to pull her boots on last night, the ones with the tall heels and the pointed toes she'd found at the thrift shop. "My dancin' shoes," she'd said as she stomped a two-step around the bed, all the way out the door and down the steps. Billie remembered thinking, only two drinks, and Ma will be at The Ball, and she'll have transformed Roger into a Dashing Prince. *What had gone wrong?*

Billie dug her nails into her thighs and kept her breathing slow, measured. "Is she in the hospital?"

Roger stared at his hands. "My mama lived in fairy tales," he mumbled, seemingly unaware that his nose was running, dripping onto his lips.

"She sang pretty songs to me . . . till they took her away . . ."

Billie's eyes frantically searched the counters, certain there would be an open liquor bottle. Roger was obviously in a stupor, muttering about his mother, who Billie had never heard him mention ever before.

Billie bent toward him, trying to get his eyes to see her. "*My* mother, Roger—where is *my* mother?"

Roger snuffled, but made no move to wipe his nose. "Dead," he said, his voice as flat and lifeless as the word itself.

"No, Ma's not dead." She spoke slowly and clearly, so Roger would hear her. "Don't worry, Roger; it's somebody else the cops found. Cops make mistakes all the time."

Roger slammed his fist on the table. The saucer with the smoldering cigarette butt clattered to the floor, and Billie trembled. Roger ground his work boot on the linoleum, pulverizing the cigarette. "~~Damn~~, stupid, foolish woman!" he shouted. "No different from my own crazy mother. Never knew when to say quit!"

Billie leaped from the table and grabbed Roger's shirt, just below the writing on the pocket. "What are you talking about? ~~Damn it~~, Roger!

Go to the station and tell the cops it's not my mother!"

Roger pulled Billie's hand from his shirt. "It *is* your ma. I saw her, kid. On a slab, ~~in the morgue.~~ Ya wanna know all the details, I'll *tell* ya!"

"Yeah!" she screamed, pounding her fists against his ugly gray shirt. "Yeah! You tell me everything, Roger—including why you came home last night and Ma didn't. Tell me why you slept like a baby while Ma was out in the night alone—getting *killed*!" Billie dropped to the floor and curled around her duffle bag. She held her breath and kept her eyes squeezed shut until she heard Roger's feet move away from the table.

"I gotta go to the station," he said. "Fill out forms, I guess. Thank God somebody saw the bastard, or I'd probably be in jail."

Billie pulled her duffle bag closer to her churning stomach and pushed her fist against her mouth to hold the sobs inside until Roger left.

She lay on the floor until the afternoon darkened into evening and the howling wind blew through the cracks around the window. When she stood, her legs felt bruised and her fingers were numb. The hands on the kitchen clock moved past 5:30. Ma should be in the kitchen right now, stirring something on the stove, telling Billie, "Quit complaining! Leftover stew's better than no dinner at all." Oh, Ma, Billie thought; if only you were here. I'd never complain about supper again. I'd eat stew a hundred nights in a row. . . .

A sour taste rose in Billie's mouth as she tried to swallow back new tears. No more leftover stew. No more foolish tale-spinning. No more Ma. She felt the reality trodding like an enemy army through her insides, leaving bruises all over her heart and screaming in her head. No more Ma. *No more Ma.* She clapped her hands over her ears. "Shut up!" she yelled. When she pulled her hands away, the screaming was gone from her head, but the bruises still throbbed.

She remembered when she'd fallen down the steps when she was little. Ma had said, "It's only a bruise, Billie. Don't make a big deal about it." What would Ma say about this bruise? Billie wondered.

Now it was after 6:00. If Ma was here, she'd be urging Billie to get at her homework. Billie ran cold water in the kitchen sink and held the wet dishrag on her face. "It's only a bruise, Billie," she told herself, even though she knew it was a lie.

She spread her math papers on her bed. She could feel the plastic dancers silently watching from the dresser as she scribbled and erased numbers until her paper was splotched and torn. She shoved the math book onto the floor and tried to write her social studies outline. A pile of crumpled notebook paper collected at her feet. Finally, she tossed her pencil across the room. As it bounced against the dresser, she wondered if Roger would come home tonight—or ever.

She stuffed the unfinished homework back into her duffle, then pulled her sketch pad from under her mattress. "A secret present from an elf," Ma told her the day after Christmas. "No need to mention it to Roger, right?" She winked, and Billie's heart felt like it was going to explode with thank-yous. She hadn't drawn one picture after Roger went on his rampage in November, screaming at Ma and tearing up every one of Billie's pictures he could find.

"The kid don't do nothin' useful! Starin' out the window—followin' us with her eyes while she scratches like a chicken with that ~~damn~~ pencil—"

Billie felt fire behind her eyes as Ma just stood there, watching Roger rip and crumble the pictures she'd claimed to love. Billie ran to her room and pulled a pillow over her head to keep her sobs private, but when the kitchen door slammed, Ma sat on Billie's bed.

"You don't have to stop drawin', Baby," Ma said. "I'll figure something out."

Billie hadn't expected Ma to remember her promise.

Now Billie's fingers caressed the pencil lines in the first picture she'd drawn on the new sketch pad, lingering on Ma's smile.

"You draw me so young and pretty," Ma said when she saw the drawing. "Maybe that's what bothers Roger. You keep that one safe, you hear? I'd rather look at your pictures than in the mirror!"

Billie poised her pencil above the thick paper. She studied the music box couple until her hand began to move. She added a Christmas tree, and Ma dancing, in the background. She scribbled the date at the bottom of the picture, and stowed the pad back under the mattress. Before she shut off the bedroom light, Billie turned the knob on the bottom of the music box.

As the music chimed and set the couple to dancing, Billie slid under the bedcovers, still dressed in her school clothes. She cradled the music box in her arms, and listened in the darkness for Ma's singing to rise from the little plastic box with the tinkling music. And she heard it: *There's a magical someplace with songs to sing.* But the words sounded hollow, empty.

"Some dreams just don't take," Ma once told her. "Then, you gotta dream up some new ones." But Ma never told Billie how to get new dreams started.

THREE

Billie turned from the window, from the trees and telephone poles and lighted signs that blurred in the darkness as Roger pressed his foot harder on the gas pedal.

"Kee-rist," he muttered, scowling over the steering wheel. "Dim yer ~~damn~~ lights."

Billie watched the bright beam shine across the top of Roger's Minnesota Vikings cap as the car passed by. Roger swore again, then glanced across at Billie.

"What are you starin' at?" he asked.

"Nothing," Billie said. She turned back to the darkness and the fast-fleeing shapes out the window. In the months since Ma died, Billie worked hard to paralyze her heart. After the funeral, Roger wiped his nose with the back of his hand, walked away from the grave, and said, "That's that." He looked her straight in the eyes and told her, "Cryin' won't bring back the dead, kid." She knew then that she'd have to learn how to stop feeling Ma inside her.

She practiced every night, thinking of things she missed now that Ma was gone. At first, just one little memory of picking summer daisies pressed on the bruises, and Billie would cry until she could barely breathe. But she learned how to take deep breaths to hold back the tears, and she repeated, over and over again, "It's only a bruise." Soon, she could see moving pictures in her memory of Ma laughing and singing and dancing, and she didn't feel the slightest little pinch in her heart, unless she stopped holding her breath.

She had tried, too, to find the "good daddy" Ma thought was somewhere inside Roger. As Ma had told her many times, he bought groceries, and they never once got kicked out of an apartment because they couldn't make the rent.

"So he yells," Ma had said, looking hard into Billie's eyes. "All fathers yell."

Looking at Roger's reflection in her window, Billie thought that if there was an ounce of good father in him, it was the best-kept secret in the universe. As he slammed his fist against the steering wheel and sent cigarette ashes flying, she couldn't keep hoping that cooking his favorite foods and trying to stay out of his way would transform him.

"Gimme some chips, kid," Roger said.

Billie felt around the floor of the pickup. "None left," she said, crumpling the bag.

Roger flung his arm across the seat and snatched the bag from her hands. The truck swerved as he smashed the bag against the seat between them. When his stare returned to the road, it seemed his angry, turned-down mouth yanked his eyebrows down, too, making a furry hood over his eyes. Billie folded her arms across her chest and stared at the dashboard clock, permanently fixed at 2:10. Why was Roger so mad at her? He was the pig who ate them all!

It was past 11:00 when Roger turned the car into a gas station and shut off the engine. "Do what you gotta do," he said, "then get back to the truck."

Billie headed around the side of the building. Behind her, Roger mumbled as he unscrewed the gas cap. When she came out of the ladies' room, he hollered to her, "Wait in the truck."

The neon sign blinked against the darkness around the dingy gas station, casting eerie shadows on the big office window. Billie could see Roger leaning against a far wall inside. He took a bottle from the man behind the counter, and raised it to his lips. After he handed the bottle back, the sound of his thick laughter floated out the door and in through Billie's cracked window.

She climbed out of the pickup and glanced at the heaps of stuff in the back of the truck. Another move; another new school. And who knew how many miles farther now from Ma's grave? Her "eternal home" the preacher had said when he threw dirt into the hole, and Billie had thought: At least you don't have to move anymore, Ma.

She gazed across the upturned chairs and cardboard boxes. Roger's junk. Why he bothered to drag it along to a new town was a real mystery to Billie. Ma used to take useless stuff with her when she moved on, too. But Billie wouldn't take old furniture and faded curtains when she ran away. No, she knew what was really important; she planned to travel light.

She pushed the heavy glass door open and stepped into the dusty office. "Um, Roger," she said. "Are we gonna get going soon?"

Roger took the bottle from the guy wearing the dirty coveralls. "Mason" was embroidered over one chest pocket.

"Can't you see that Mason and I are *social- izin'*?" he said.

"I'm tired," Billie whined. "Are we going to get a motel room?"

"If you're tired, girl, go sleep in the truck. I ain't ready to leave yet." He waved the bottle under her nose. "Maybe you'd like to socialize, too?"

Billie wrinkled her nose. "I don't think so," she said. "But I am thirsty. Could I have a soda?"

"Go on, you old cheapskate," Mason said. "Give your kid some soda pop from the cooler over there."

"She ain't *my* kid," Roger said, opening the cooler door. He tossed two cans to Billie. "Now, git back to the truck!"

Outside the office, she shivered. April in Minnesota barely hinted at spring. Zipping her parka, she heard Roger tell Mason, "My old lady died a few months ago, and I got stuck with her brat."

Back in the truck, Billie scraped frost from the window with her fingernail. With Roger inside the gas station, *socializing*, she'd have plenty of time to gather her things and be on her way before he'd even notice she was gone.

And then what? Would he report her to the police? Would her picture be splattered across the front pages of newspapers and displayed on national television? Roger's words were fresh in Billie's mind. *"I got stuck with her brat."* It wasn't the first time she'd heard him say that; he'd be glad to have her out of the way. And he hadn't registered her at a new school yet, so he'd have nothing to explain to anyone if Billie disappeared.

Billie smiled. School had always been the biggest problem with get-away plans. Roger might not care if Billie left, but the school officials would ask questions. When she and Ma had moved to a town in Ohio, Ma forgot to tell the Iowa school that they were moving. Actually, Ma suddenly decided to move in the middle of the night, in the middle of a week. She told Billie it would be "an adventure." Five weeks later, some people came knocking at their apartment. They said they were "checking on Billie's safety," but Ma said they were just nosy people from the government. There wouldn't be any nosy people this time, she thought.

Roger sat, and leaned his back against the display window. If there was ever a right time to escape, this was it.

Billie crouch-walked to the rear of the truck. For weeks she had been scrounging up odd bits of rope and fishing line, matches and Band-Aids, stashing them into her duffle. Just the other day, she'd found a book on the 25-cent rack at the library: *Field Guide: Incredible Edibles of the Midwest*. It was old and smelled like dirt, but if a dream ever called her, she planned to be ready to follow it, no matter where it might take her.

The gas station sign blinked on, but just as Billie spied the duffle among the jumble of chairs, old motors, tools and suitcases, the sign blinked off. She waited a few minutes, until she found a rhythm in the off-on blinking. She pulled her things from the pickup when the light flickered on the gas pumps, and checked Roger's position when the sign was dark. Once everything was heaped on the ground, she knew she'd never be able to carry it all.

Filled with her Emergency Escape Items and her sketching things, the duffle pack was a necessity. So was the sleeping bag, with the extra clothing and the quilt Ma made rolled inside. She held Ma's photo album and sighed. It was bulky, but it was full of Ma's memories. How could she leave it for Roger to toss into a dumpster later on? Quickly she flipped through it, blindly pulled snapshots from the pages, then tossed the album back into the pickup.

Sliding across the worn seat cover, she fumbled with the glove compartment. She banged it with her fist the way Roger did it, and it popped open. Billie lingered, just a moment, wondering if God would punish her for stealing. Not if He knows Roger, she told herself, plucking several bills from Roger's money clip. She jiggled the glove compartment shut and squeezed the sodas into her cloth purse.

Roger was walking toward the men's room. If she didn't get moving fast, her plan was doomed. And so was she. She slipped out of the truck and hoisted the pack to her shoulders. It felt heavier than it had when she'd carried it to the truck this morning. She kept her eyes steady on the men's room door as she backed across the asphalt lot and dropped into the weeds beside the highway. She looked down the winding road, and tried to figure out which way Roger would go when he left the station. She was sure he'd be heading south.

"I'm gettin' outta this ~~frozen hell~~," he'd said a month ago when a surprise storm dumped a foot of snow out of the sky. He'd shaken Billie awake before daylight had even broken through the tiny window in her bedroom. "Where's the shovel?" he shouted. A fine mist of spit sprayed through his teeth.

He grabbed her by the shoulders and raised her upright in the bed. "Where's the shovel?" he said again, his red-rimmed eyes glaring into hers.

"I-I-I don't know," Billie told him. "You used it when you got the truck stuck over by Leroy's bar."

Roger let go of her shoulders and raised his right arm above his head. Billie cringed, and slid closer to the wall, but Roger didn't hit her. He just punched the air between them and turned toward the door. "I'm gettin' outta this frozen ~~hole~~." He looked over his shoulder at her and smiled. "Maybe I'll go all the way to Flor'da!" He slapped his knee. "Now there's an idea; I'll maybe go down t' Flor'da and work in Greg's garage." He seemed to be talking to himself. Billie didn't know anybody named Greg from Florida.

Before she could ask him about that, the smile left his face. "Git outta that bed and find me the ~~damn~~ shovel." He banged his fist against the door-jamb, and left the room.

Crouched in the weeds, Billie heard Roger leave the men's room. She held her breath until the muffled sounds of conversation and laughter assured her that Roger was back inside with Mason. Roger hadn't bothered to say where they were going when he told her to pack, but Billie thought it was a safe bet that he was heading them toward Greg's garage.

Just beyond the weeds was a highway marker. COUNTY 17 SOUTH. She raced across the road, down into the ravine, and headed north.

Thin sheets of ice crackled under her canvas

sneakers. The tall, frost-stiff reeds made high-pitched whistle sounds as they brushed against her jeans and jacket. She sprinted into the darkness without slowing her pace, even when every breath she sucked in began to burn in her chest. Instinctively, she timed herself, glancing now and then at the lighted dial on her watch. If she concentrated hard and visualized the second-hand sweeping rhythmically around the face of her watch, she could make herself lift her feet, even though they felt like concrete blocks as the miles between her and Roger increased.

Every time headlights appeared, Billie's heart jumped into her throat, but she kept on running in the shadowed gully, not sure what she'd do if a truck stopped and Roger scrambled out the door. As the beams disappeared into the night, she was glad Ma had started spinning runner's dreams into her head long ago. She'd been only seven or eight when Ma watched her chase across the park after a squirrel. "Such long legs!" Ma said when Billie returned, breathless. "You could be a track star—maybe even go to the Olympics some day!" The dream was planted then and there, and Billie had been running every day since that summer afternoon. Now, if she thought about how the sun sometimes fell on her hair and shoulders when she ran in the summertime, she could stay warm for a hundred yards or more, even though her panting left thick clouds in the air.

When the long stretch of weedy ravines abruptly ended, Billie stopped to catch her breath and consider how to keep moving without being seen. There really weren't any options, she realized. She shifted her pack higher up on her back. She put her head down and sprinted past the straight-aways and places where driveways and other roads connected, not slowing until another trench or stand of trees appeared along the shoulder of the road.

Four hours later, she smiled. Maybe Roger really wasn't going to come after her. But in spite of eyelids that wanted to close and muscles that ached, Billie knew she couldn't stop yet. A few more hours, she told herself, rubbing her icy fingers across her temples. From someplace in the darkness came a wild cry, a mournful howl that sent chills shivering along Billie's spine. She quickened her pace.

On and on she plodded, her feet squishing in her now-soaked sneakers, until the blue-black sky became streaked with light grays and blues, like spongy art paper slowly splashed with a watercolor wash. Soon there wouldn't be any night shadows to hide in.

As the first rays of day broke through the gray sky, the frosted grasses and trees and highway signs shimmered. Maybe it was her imagination, but it seemed the sun shined brighter on one sign than any of the others. GAS FOOD LODGING.

"You up there, God?" she said, shielding her eyes as she looked smack into the sunlight. Ma told her that God left messages for people, but most folks didn't know how to read them. Ma read notes from God in some of the strangest places.

Before following the sign, Billie scanned the gully twice. She didn't want to take too much gear into town; someone might question why a kid was hauling everything she owned on her back. The culvert would be a good place to stow her sleeping bag and backpack, if it didn't rain. She watched the sunshine flicker on the metal drainage pipe. "Right, God," she said. "No rain today."

It was a relief to walk without the heavy burden of the pack; without the cumbersome lump of sleeping bag bumping against her side. She strode along the side of the road, her head held high and her purse swinging beside her. She hoped she looked like she knew where she was going. Mostly she looked straight ahead, but occasionally, she'd smile at the vague person-shapes inside an oncoming car. It helped her to feel less alone.

At the first gas station in town, the ladies' room was locked. Shifting from one foot to the other, she waited for the person inside to leave. Ten minutes later, she put her ear to the door, then walked around to the front of the building.

"The bathroom is locked," she told the lady at the cash register.

"Right," the lady said, reaching under the counter. "You need this." She handed Billie a key attached to a looped rough rope.

"Thanks," said Billie.

The toilet sounded like it could swallow up entire countries when it was flushed, and the water only dribbled out of the sink faucet. But Billie was able to wash her face and brush her teeth. Then she dropped the toilet lid and sat down to count the bills she'd taken from Roger's truck.

"Omigosh!" she said, paging through the bills one more time. It was more than she'd hoped for, and maybe *too* much. Would Roger think that $215.00 was a small price to pay to get rid of Carolyn Rowe's brat? Or would he decide to report the theft, and let the cops send Billie to jail? It was hard telling what Roger would do. Billie figured she'd have to lay low for a while, just in case.

But now, she thought, I have *money*—and I can *eat!* She returned the key to the lady at the counter, then bought a pack of gum, some peanut butter cheese crackers and a three-pack of apple juice to add to her duffle bag stash. She grinned as she took the small bag and headed down the sidewalk to a café near the bakery.

The waitress frowned over tortoise-shell glasses at Billie. "Are you *alone*?" she asked.

"Yes—er—I'm—" Billie searched for words that would sound reasonable. "I'm—uh—meeting my father," Billie said.

"Okay. Y'want t'wait for him before you order?"

"Um, no. I eat kind of slow, so I can start ahead of him." Billie smiled up at the waitress. "I want pancakes and sausage. And a giant glass of milk."

"Comin' right up, young lady." The waitress whooshed through the swinging kitchen door.

"The plate's hot," she said, setting the steaming plate in front of Billie.

The aroma of buckwheat and sausage rose from the plate and warmed Billie's face. She painted the pancakes with butter and stuffed a sausage link into her mouth. The waitress was still standing beside the table as Billie reached for the chrome syrup pitcher.

"Don't look like you're a slow eater t'me," the waitress said. She looked toward the door. "You sure your father's coming to join you?"

Billie pushed the sausage to one side in her mouth. "Yeah," she said. "He'll be here any time now."

"Oaky doaky, kid. Whatever you say." She scribbled something on her pad and clicked her tongue as she walked away, jingling coins in her apron pocket.

Probably worried about her tip, Billie thought, picking up her fork. The waitress continued to peer through the small window in the swinging door, so Billie made herself eat slowly. Before she finished her milk, the waitress was beside the table. "Looks like *Daddy* isn't gonna show," the waitress said, tapping the pad with her pen.

"His loss." Billie smiled. "The food was great!" She opened her wallet. "Do I pay here, or up front?"

The waitress cleared her throat and flashed a toothpaste-commercial smile as she handed Billie the check. "I'll be glad to take care of it for you, honey."

Billie took her time checking the addition before she laid a ten dollar bill on the plastic tray. While the waitress worked the cash register, Billie put on her coat. Ma always said Billie was thrifty. Now that skill would pay off in spades. Her stomach was filled to the brim, and she was only out $2.59.

Her mind returned to the highway and her belongings in the culvert, but she paused outside a small grocery store. She should buy more food, in case she wasn't near a town again for a while.

The cashier smiled as he rung up the prices and put an apple, a banana, an orange, and a large box of raisins in a bag. "A real fruit lover, eh?" he said.

"Uh-huh," Billie mumbled.

"Better hurry," the man said, nodding toward the door, "or you'll be late for school. Have a nice day!"

Outside, school buses were lined up at the traffic light. No need to worry about the tardy bell today, she thought. No need to worry about school bells at all.

The sun was bright now, shining on skimpy patches of snow left on the fields and hillsides. But it was a cold shimmer, and though there wasn't much of a breeze, icy air made her nose and cheeks sting. She increased her pace, stuffing her hands into the pockets of her parka; she wished she hadn't left her gloves on the seat of the pickup.

Back at the culvert, she squeezed into the big pipe with her gear. It was cramped, but she wriggled about until she was able to dig her pad and pencil from the duffle. She thumbed through it until she came to a blank page. Quickly her pencil sketched the view from the tin cave. As she drew, she thought of the journals sailors kept when they made long ocean voyages.

April 19, she wrote below the picture. *I did it. I got away from Roger. I'm still in Minnesota, but soon I'll be living with* . . . She lifted her pencil and gave her mind some time to try dream-making. . . . *I'll be living with Great Aunt Gloria in a huge white house with black shutters and a real front yard.*

Billie rubbed the eraser across her teeth. She hadn't thought about Ma's aunt for a long time. She wondered why she'd written about her now. She smiled. During the months she'd been hoping for a dream to escape into, she planned carefully, making sure she had a Swiss army knife, first aid supplies, and other important things she'd seen people pack when they went camping. But she hadn't once thought about where she would go if she ever got away from Roger. Getting away had seemed too impossible to carry the fantasy any farther.

But now, it really was as if God had spoken to her, making her fingers scribble out Great Aunt Gloria's name beneath a picture of highway litter tucked among tall blowing grass. *God?* Sending her *three* messages in one day, when He'd never sent her *any* messages before? Not likely, she thought, but however it happened, it *is* something of a miracle.

Great Aunt Gloria's was the perfect place to go. The *only* place to go. Ma never talked about any other relatives, at least not with any fondness, but when she spoke of her Aunt Gloria, her eyes would sparkle like the blue stones in the jewelry at the drug store.

Billie was five when she first heard about Gloria. Ma had been washing Billie's hair in a truck stop bathroom, on their way to another new town.

"The first time I met her, Aunt Gloria had five pure gold bracelets dangling from one arm," Ma said, her voice drifting off to a space beyond Billie's sudsy hair. " . . . a long, flowing skirt and high boots . . ."

Billie looked in the mirror above the sink; even in the dingy glass, Ma's eyes were shining. Billie reached up to catch the suds on her forehead, and Ma took a paper cup from the holder above the sink. She poured rinse water over Billie's head.

"Aunt Gloria was your grandma's younger sister. She played the guitar and sang lovely, sad songs on the porch steps at night. My mother didn't much like the songs any more than she liked Gloria's skirts and boots, but I tried to memorize the words and the tunes—songs about soldiers and love blowing away 'like dandelions and dust in a tear storm.'" Ma sang the last few words, then wrapped a long ribbon of paper towel around Billie's head.

"Yes, Aunt Gloria was something," she said. "As different from my mother as an iris is from ragweed." She laughed then. "Funny thing is, my mother thought Aunt Gloria was the ragweed."

Billie stashed the pad back in her duffle. She didn't know if Great Aunt Gloria had a white house with black shutters, but if God had made her write the words, she supposed He knew what sort of house Aunt Gloria lived in. Billie remembered Ma saying that Aunt Gloria "took in every stray cat and dog that wandered into her yard." A lady who worried about homeless animals, Billie reasoned, would surely find room for her dead niece's child.

Billie pulled the quilt from inside the sleeping bag and scooted farther into the drainage pipe.

"She brought me a little porcelain doll that first time," Ma told Billie. "Imagine, she'd been all the way to Germany to buy things for her gift shop business."

With the bunched-up quilt as a lumpy pillow, Billie curled into the sleeping bag and closed her eyes. As the sounds of highway traffic whirred down into the gully, Billie wondered if Great Aunt Gloria still went to Germany for china dolls; if she still knew the song about the dandelions in a tear storm. Ma knew only that one line, nothing more. Maybe Great Aunt Gloria would teach Billie all the words. Maybe. But Billie didn't know where to even begin to look for Ma's Aunt Gloria.

FOUR

Four lanes of traffic droned their tuneless songs as Billie tramped through the third night along more highway ditches. She felt the darkness of the marsh slinking toward her, and shadows of branches, moving under the moonlight, reached across the gully like thick, trembling arms. She wondered how many nights it would take before she'd no longer be spooked by sounds and sights she couldn't recognize.

The fast-moving lights from the highway sent momentary brightness onto the path ahead. It was a nice balance, Billie decided; the illusion of daytime even as the shadowed darkness kept her hidden. But as the miles passed behind her and real daylight began to swallow up the stars, Billie searched for a place to sleep. She'd hoped for another abandoned house, like the one she'd found yesterday. Even though all the windows were shattered, the sun made a warm spot for her to sleep undiscovered on the living room floor.

But there weren't any houses along this stretch of road; only groups of houses, off in the distance, and all of them appeared to be new and probably lived-in.

Soon, all of the stars had disappeared, and still she hadn't spotted a safe hiding place. Across the highway, the sun hovered over the top of a billboard. SUNRISE MALL. 22 STORES UNDER ONE ROOF. ONE MILE AHEAD. The sun was rising right over the Sunrise Mall advertisement!

"Boy, God, you sure have some great ideas," she said, and hurried to follow the directions.

She had to wait behind some shrubs near the parking lot until the mall opened at nine. She curled up in the middle of the stiff, prickly branches and thought about the Food Court sign over one section of the building. She giggled. What would she find in that "court"? Sinful sweets? Fast food—so fast, it exceeds the speed limit? Tacos spicy enough to turn your breath into a lethal weapon? Billie covered her mouth to silence her laughter. Maybe a Confiscated Cookie Joint—with trays full of cookies shaped like guns and rifles and knives and . . .

Billie stopped laughing and smashed the knife-cookie her imagination had baked. She wouldn't go to the Confiscated Cookie place, even if it was there in the Food Court. A cookie shaped like a knife wouldn't be fun to eat.

She hadn't let herself think about the night Ma got stabbed for a long time, and she wished she hadn't thought about it now. Roger said the guy who killed Ma was "stupid."

"He could've just stolen her purse and been done with it," Roger said, "and he probably never would've gotten caught." Billie figured the guy was worse than just stupid—probably crazy. She wondered if you could tell if someone was a murderer just by looking at them. If someone wanted to kill *her*, would she know it in time to run away?

She shivered, and the prickly branches clawed at her face, reminding her that she was waiting for the mall to open. It would be a safe place to rest, and she wouldn't have to worry about murderers. She left her sleeping bag in the shrubbery, but took her duffle. Lots of kids carried duffles everywhere, so that wouldn't look odd.

Although her stomach rumbled from hunger, Billie let herself get side-tracked at the toy store. She walked past the cashier and headed down an aisle.

"Young lady!" the cashier called out.

Billie turned. "Me?"

"Yeah, you. Can't ya read?" She pointed to a

sign on the counter. LEAVE ALL PACKAGES AND
SCHOOL BAGS WITH CLERK.

"Oh, sorry," Billie replied, hoisting her duffle
onto the counter.

The lady gave her a cardboard number. "Turn
in the card when you leave, kiddo, and you get
your stuff back."

Billie passed by the teen dolls and a whole row
of clothes to fit them. On one shelf, farther down
the aisle, were brightly colored plastic bracelets
and rings, and a box full of tiny baby dolls. "Neat,"
Billie said, snapping one of the little dolls onto a
purple bracelet, and slipping the bracelet over her
wrist. She smiled. She'd have liked one of these
when she was younger. A miniature friend to stay
with her, night and day, no matter where she and
Ma moved. She put the bracelet back on the shelf
and moved on.

At the end of the doll aisle was a glass case.
Billie counted twenty-two porcelain dolls, all
shapes and sizes, standing in metal holders on
the glass shelves. Did Aunt Gloria give Ma a doll
like one of these? A baby doll, with glass-blue
eyes? A bride doll, complete with satin dress and
lace veil? Billie wished she had seen Ma's doll.
She had to bend down and peer up through the
bottom of the shelves to see the prices. The

cheapest one was $85.00, but some cost $350.00! If Aunt Gloria gave Billie a porcelain doll, she'd take special care of it, so she could give it to her own little girl some day.

Around the corner, Billie spied a small, pink piano. It took several tries, but finally she was able to *plink-plink* the "dandelions and dust in a tear storm" tune. She could remember the Aunt Gloria tunes Ma had sung; why couldn't she think of where Aunt Gloria lived? Billie slapped both of her hands against the little piano keys.

"Eh-hem, Miss!"

The desk lady stood rigid in front of her, her hands pressed tightly against her hips. "If you're not buying, don't handle the merchandise."

"I—wanted to—*test* it," Billie said.

"And?" The lady's eyebrows looked like lying-down question marks. "Shall I ring it up for you?"

"I have to think about it," Billie replied. She handed the lady the cardboard number and hoisted her duffle over her shoulder as she left the store.

Out in the mall, food aromas led her to the Food Court. As she walked among the food stands, checking the menus and prices posted on the walls, she laughed. There were no weapon-shaped cookies in this place, but the prices sure were criminal.

The oatmeal cookies at the Bakery Boutique

were the size of sandwich plates, and they smelled just as wonderful as the little ones Ma sometimes made. Billie took a dollar from her wallet while the boy with the white apron put a cookie into a bag. She stuffed the five-cents change into her jeans and headed for the ice cream place.

"A pineapple sundae," she said. "Um-m, can I have whipped cream and nuts and cherries, too?"

The gray-haired lady smiled beneath her red-striped visor. "Not a very healthy breakfast, my dear." She winked.

Billie smiled back. "Sure it is," she said. "Frozen milk—fruit for vitamins—and nuts are protein, right?"

The lady laughed. "I never thought of it like that before." She piled scoops of pineapple and cherries on top of the huge ice cream mound and eyed Billie's bakery bag. "But a cookie? How's that breakfast?"

Billie slipped the cookie from the bag and held it up. "A bowl of oatmeal, extra crispy!"

The lady squirted a spiral mountain of whipped cream onto the fruit. "And here's some extra calcium. Enjoy!"

She watched all the while Billie ate the sundae and the cookie, and the smile never left her face. When Billie scraped the last of the ice cream from the plastic dish and pulled her duffle off the bench, the lady handed her a cup of ice water.

"You'll be thirsty soon; take this along."

"Thanks," Billie said. "It was the best breakfast I've had in days!"

By eleven o'clock, Billie had passed each of the twenty-two stores at least once. It was a bother to check her duffle just to look at clothes and gadgets she couldn't buy anyway, so she only window-shopped. But at the pet store, it was worth the hassle to have both hands free to pet the puppies and cuddle the kittens. One of the kittens in a case labeled AMERICAN DOMESTICS looked exactly like the one she'd wished for at Christmastime. If only she knew where to find Aunt Gloria, she'd gladly have paid the fifteen dollars to buy the kitten. Aunt Gloria would surely let Billie have a pet.

"Bye, Dusty," she said, gently setting the gray kitten back in the cage. Her heart was as heavy as her duffle when she left the store.

She yawned, and remembered why God had sent her to the mall. Window shopping was only tiring out her feet, and she'd need some sleep to continue her journey when night came. She'd passed The Cove several times as she'd wandered around the mall; telephones, vending machines and rest rooms, all in one convenient location.

Planning now for a meal that would wait in her duffle for later, she stopped at the vending machines. The quarters *plink-plinked* on their way through the slot, finally clanging softly to announce the end of their journey. Billie studied the selections while she rubbed her legs. She wished she could reach the end of her travels as quickly as the quarters did. She wished she at least knew where her journey would end.

The ladies' room wasn't crowded. Two teenagers were bent over the sinks, staring like zombies into the mirrors as they dabbed bright pink shadow on their eyelids and blue mascara on their lashes.

"We got a real deal on *this* make-up, huh?" the red-haired girl said, giggling.

"Shush!" the girl with black curls hissed, glancing at Billie. "Ya never know when a snitch is listening."

Billie stepped to another sink and clamped her duffle between her feet. She pumped soap from the dispenser into her palm and reached for the faucet knobs. There weren't any! The sink was broken. She looped her foot through one of the duffle handles and shuffled to the next sink. That sink was broken, too! The make-up thieves were watching and smiling.

"You drop outta the sky from Mars or somethin'?" The red-haired girl snickered. "Hi-tech bathrooms in *this* world," she said. She shoved her hand under Billie's faucet. Water magically appeared!

Billie tried it. Warm water sprayed onto her hands. When she pulled her hands away, the water stopped instantly. "Awesome!" she said.

The girls were still laughing when they left.

Now the bathroom was empty. Billie used the toilet, then dropped the lid and rested her duffle against the back of the tank. She'd have liked to curl her legs under her, but she figured it was better to leave her feet showing in case anyone peeked under the door. To rest her head, she had to arch her back uncomfortably. Maybe she wouldn't even be able to sleep in this twisted position, but she had to try. She closed her eyes and listened to the bathroom. The entry door swished open regularly, often bringing conversation and laughter bouncing around the tile walls; stall doors banged shut, toilets flushed, stall doors clicked open, water lapped like soft ocean waves in the magic sinks, and the drying machines sent warm spring breeze sounds to Billie's ears. A baby cried, and a lady's voice softly crooned, "Okay, sweetie. Off with that soggy

COYOTE GIRL   57

diaper." She began to sing nursery rhymes, and the baby quieted. Sometime during the singing, Billie fell asleep.

Hours later, a loud thumping startled Billie.

"Hey! You okay in there?"

The words were hollered, right outside Billie's stall.

As Billie pulled her head off the duffle, a sharp pain shot down her neck and settled into her shoulders.

"Ugh!" she grunted, then cleared her throat. "Um, yeah. I'm okay." White shoes, like nurses' shoes, poked half-way under the door.

"I gotta clean here, kid. You sick?"

Billie looked at her watch. Holy cow! She'd been sleeping for nearly six hours!

"If'n you need help, I'll git Officer Stephan."

Billie grabbed her duffle and purse and unlocked the door. She gave the uniformed lady with the multi-colored hair a weak smile. "I, uh, must have eaten too much junk. My ma says never to overdo a good thing." Billie shrugged and babbled on. "I guess she's right." She brushed past the cleaning lady and headed for the exit.

The lady held the door open. "Junk food overload, that's all," she yelled into the corridor. "Everything's under control, Stephan."

Officer Stephan bounced the black stick hooked to his belt against his thigh as Billie came out of the rest room. His eyes studied her face, moved to her duffle, and continued all the way down to her shoes.

Billie wrapped her arms dramatically across her stomach. "Too many peanuts, I think. Sorry if I worried you."

The policeman frowned and pulled a photo book from an inside pocket of his jacket. He flipped through the pictures, then nodded. "Okay, pal. Better head on home now."

"Right," Billie replied.

When she was able to sneak her sleeping bag from the shrubs and find a side road to travel, her breathing finally slowed. What if *her* picture had been in that officer's book? What then?

If she couldn't figure out where to find Aunt Gloria, she'd have to think of some other plan. Maybe God would come through with the answers soon. She sure hoped that her Aunt Gloria dream wasn't one of those dreams Ma had talked about—the kind that "don't take." For now, it was the only plan she had.

FIVE

Dusk gave way to darkness, and the air grew damp and cold as the highway ended and Billie followed a winding, narrow road. She stopped worrying now about whether Roger had called the police about his stolen money. If he'd reported her missing, surely Officer Stephan wouldn't have let her leave the mall.

Light drizzle changed to sleet. It stabbed at Billie's face as she slipped along the shoulder of the road. Few cars were out in the storm, but as the sleet melted into her parka and sneakers, Billie wished a car would come by. This time, she wouldn't scramble to hide, like she'd been doing the past three nights. She'd face the headlights and try to look helpless. And the people in the car would be a nice old couple who would feed her and give her a warm place to sleep and help her find Great Aunt Gloria.

Great Aunt Gloria. Ever since she'd written that peculiar sentence in her sketchbook she'd been trying to think of whether Ma ever said where Gloria lived. But so far, all Billie could remember was Ma talking about the gold bracelets and how Aunt Gloria was the iris of the family.

Billie rearranged the backpack and the sleeping bag so she could hold the hood of her parka around her face and still keep walking. Hunched over, it was nearly impossible to see where she was going. She guessed there wasn't much to see anyway, except gravel and the eerie shadows of trees and fields beside a road that stretched on forever.

Even the moon and the night creatures know better than to be out on a night like this, Billie thought. Her teeth chattered as icy dampness crept through the layers of her clothing, and she could no longer feel her fingers gripping the hood. She willed herself to keep moving, hoping that soon the lights from a gas station or a tavern would glow on the horizon. She fought the tears that pressed against her eyelids as she looked through the darkness for someplace to hole up until the storm passed. Soon she'd have to stop, even if she didn't find a dry shelter.

Why wasn't God sending messages now, when she really needed them? After all of the blisters she'd accumulated, and all of her keeping-on when her legs wanted to quit, was this how her dream would end? In the middle of nowhere, with the sleet covering her until she was frozen?

She thought about who might happen along in the morning and find her sealed in ice, like the little snowman figurine she'd once seen in a glass globe. But whoever found her wouldn't be able to shake the globe she'd be in, and make snowflakes flutter about.

"I should have known this would never work!" Billie shouted. "My luck's no better than Ma's." She left the gravel shoulder and pressed her back against the trunk of a pine tree. Its spreading long-needled branches created a canopy around her. As ice specks landed on her eyelashes, she recalled reading about an old Eskimo who sat on an ice-covered rock for days, waiting to die. But Billie didn't want to die. She hadn't broken loose of Roger and all the years of flitting from one place to another, only to die before week's end; before she found the Someplace the music box song promised. "Stupid planning," she mumbled. "Just plain stupid."

If Roger were there, he'd have said, "Empty-headed," and then he'd grind his finger into her forehead so hard she'd expect a hole to poke through and prove there were no brains inside. Before, when Roger would do that, she'd tell herself over and over that it was Roger who had no brains. . . . Roger had no brains. . . . Roger . . . But now as her jeans soaked up the wet-cold beneath her, she thought maybe Roger had been right about her all along.

She wondered if Roger had made it to Florida yet, if he was swimming in the ocean or tanning on the beach. Maybe he was eating oranges every morning on a sun-soaked balcony. If Billie had stayed with Roger, he'd be so content with the warm breezes and a new job, he wouldn't have any more meanness. Billie could be swimming and collecting seashells instead of freezing to death, still stuck in a state spring had forgotten.

She spread the sleeping bag across the crackly grass, under the pine branch roof, then crawled inside the flannel-lined pocket. Making a tent over her head with Ma's quilt, she raised up on her elbows and shined the flashlight on her last words and drawings.

Think, Billie. Think about Gloria and everything Ma told you. Rough sketches of china dolls, irises, and a guitar with gold bracelets looped through the strings filled most of the white space. At the very bottom, Billie's writing bit into the paper: *It's no use. I can't remember.*

She struggled to make her numb fingers grip the pencil, but they wouldn't close tightly enough, and the pencil kept slipping loose. She thought about the long icicles that hung from the eaves in the early winter, the ones she liked to break off and suck on as she walked to school. If she tried harder to bend her fingers, perhaps they'd snap just like those icicles. She turned off the flashlight and made pictures in her mind of what Florida would look like, and how she would look standing on the beach beside the Atlantic Ocean in a purple bathing suit.

The Atlantic Ocean! A purple bathing suit! In Ma's photo album, there had been a picture of Aunt Gloria in a purple bathing suit. On every picture in the album, Ma wrote funny sayings, or dates and names and places. Billie squeezed her eyes shut and tried to see the words under the purple bathing suit picture of Aunt Gloria. *Atlantic Ocean bathing beauty*, that was it.

In her mind's eye, Billie could see Ma's photo album as clearly as if she were paging through it. The first few pages had pictures of Ma in high school, then pictures of Ma's parents that someone had scribbled over with black marker. There were pages of pictures of people Billie didn't know, but Ma could tell long stories about each one. Usually, Billie fell asleep when Ma got to those pages; the people in the stories were rich or smart or important, but the endings were always the same. The people went away and left Ma alone again. Alone with Billie.

In the middle of the album came the Aunt Gloria pictures; first the one by the Atlantic Ocean. Ma said that someday Aunt Gloria would take them to the Atlantic Ocean and buy them each purple bathing suits, but Billie never saw Great Aunt Gloria, except in the album.

Billie bolted up from the sleeping bag and began to rummage through her duffle. With the quilt still over her head, she collected a handful of photos which had sifted to the bottom of the bag. As the sleet made flicking sounds on the quilt, she aimed the flashlight at a photo of Aunt Gloria standing beside a statue of Abraham Lincoln. *Aunt Gloria meets Abe* was scribbled in red ink. She shuffled past photos of Ma beside a green station wagon, and a picture of a vase of flowers. Next was one of Aunt Gloria with her arm around Ma. Billie remembered Ma's laughter when she came to that picture.

"The first picture of Billie Rowe," she'd say, pointing to the watermelon-sized lump under her shirt. Billie didn't laugh with Ma. There were only four pictures of Billie in the entire album, and in one of them, she was under Ma's shirt, not yet born. Billie didn't think that one should count.

Aunt Gloria wasn't wearing a long, flowing skirt in this picture, but she did have boots that went almost up to the knees of her jeans, and a bright-colored Mexican poncho. Ma went on and on about Aunt Gloria's long braids—how they were like shimmering auburn ropes that fell all the way to her waist. Billie told Ma, "If my hair was long, you could braid it like Aunt Gloria's." But Ma only said, "Your braids wouldn't be auburn, Billie."

Billie read the green-ink words under the picture: *Aunt Gloria's yard in Beacon City, Wisconsin.* She squinted in the flickering light, trying to read the sign in the photo. "Lovely sign," Ma would say, pointing to the painted flowers winding around the bold, black words. LOVELIEN LANE GIFTS, *those* were the words which took up the entire middle of the sign!

Billie leaped from the sleeping bag. "Yes!" She danced around in a small circle, then scribbled on her sketch pad: *April 21—No, it's past midnight. It's the 22nd now. Thursday, I guess. Heading off to find Beacon City, Wisconsin—and Great Aunt Gloria Lovelien!*

She'd seen a town marker awhile back; if she hurried, she could dry her gear there and get directions to Beacon City.

At 4:30 in the morning, the Quick Coin-Op laundromat was deserted. She stuffed her sleeping bag and the quilt in one dryer and the rest of the wet things into another. When the machines were humming, she made her way past the long row of washers to the rest room in the back, then lined up her shampoo, soap, toothpaste, and toothbrush on the ledge above the sink, like Ma did when they were on the move. "You want people to think you're a guttersnipe?" Ma would say as she urged Billie through sink baths in public wash rooms. Billie didn't know what that was, but she didn't think she wanted to be one. And she certainly didn't want to look and smell like a "guttersnipe" when she finally met Great Aunt Gloria.

Only the cold water faucet worked. Billie rushed through her hair-washing, hoping she hadn't left too much shampoo in her hair when her scalp became too cold for any more rinsing. Turning the hand-dryer nozzle sideways, she let the warm air blow her hair in crazy directions and take the chill from her skin.

The thumping music her clothes made in the

dryer echoed around the room. Billie climbed into the only soft chair in the place, and tucked her stocking feet underneath her. She nibbled on the vending machine sandwich she'd bought at the mall yesterday and peeled an orange. As she sucked the last of the juice off her fingers, a bent-over lady came through the door, pulling a metal wheeled cart behind her. The woman scowled at Billie, then opened the lids on three washing machines.

"Y'er in my chair," the woman said, plucking clothing from the metal cart with her gnarled fingers.

"I can move," Billie said, uncurling her legs. "I'm almost done here, anyway."

A loud, wheezing sound followed each breath the lady took, and the hump on her back moved up and down as if it were alive under the shabby tan coat. She banged the washer lids shut. "Don't leave yer trash behind when y'go." She kicked Billie's crumpled juice box away from the chair as she sat down.

Billie collected the box and the wadded sandwich paper, ignoring the old woman who had begun to mutter to herself. But she could feel the woman's eyes on her back as she rolled her sleeping bag and tied her dry tennis shoes. She set her belongings on the floor and fumbled with her parka zipper.

"You a runaway?" the woman asked.

Billie sucked in a deep breath and studied the flecks in the linoleum. Cold chills shot up her arms and settled in her back, and she began to sneeze. She cupped one hand over her nose and frantically searched her pockets with the other, hoping to find a tissue.

"Yeah, y'er a runaway, sure as I'm a crippled old woman." She dug a wallet out of her purse and unfolded a length of plastic photo sleeves. "See this here picture?" She clicked her fingernail on one of the photos.

Billie snuffed back another sneeze and inched toward the door.

"You don't need to fear me. If I mentioned seeing you this morning, folks'd just think I was having another of my visions." She laughed. "Nobody believes Martha anymore." Again she tapped the picture in her wallet. "See here, my granddaughter. Patsy was sixteen when she ran away. Sixteen when she died, too."

Billie's ma said you could tell if a person was crazy by the look in his eyes—as if his eyeballs are spinning, trying to see all the crazy thoughts whirling round in his head. Billie looked into the old woman's eyes. They were faded-green, as if time had bleached most of the color out of them, but they didn't appear to be spinning. Billie moved closer to the chair and peered at the photo, keeping a firm grasp on her gear. The girl was pretty, with long, dark hair and huge dark eyes, but her smile looked painted on.

"You gotta do what you gotta do," the old lady said, not raising her eyes. "Where are you headed?"

"Beacon City, Wisconsin," Billie replied.

"That's a far distance, child," she said. "Got a map?"

"Nope. Not yet."

The lady reached into the large, black purse, pulled out several maps, and muttered as she sorted through them. "Washington . . . West Virginia . . . Wisconsin . . . Wyoming . . ." She looked up at Billie. "Wisconsin, you say?" She thrust a neatly folded map at Billie.

"Hey, that's great!" Billie said. "Thanks!"

"Take the first right past the diner, then keep on 'til you see signs for Saliston," the lady said, staring down at the picture of Patsy. "T'ain't far. At Saliston—" The old woman paused, and Billie quickly reached for her sketch pad and pencil. "At Saliston," she repeated, "follow signs for

Wetherby, which'll put you into Wisconsin. After that, use the map."

Billie wrote furiously, hoping that Martha wasn't really crazy and just making up all those town names.

"It's about two days walking to Wetherby; I don't know how far to Beacon City after that." The woman frowned as Billie began to sneeze again. She stretched her leathery hand toward Billie, and let her fingers linger briefly on Billie's palm before she dug into her purse once more.

"If y'er not careful, you'll have pneumonia, child." She handed Billie a wad of tissues and a small green jar. "Martha's special poultice. You start feeling an ache in yer bones and the weight of a tractor on yer chest, you rub this on right away, then *stay warm*." She pressed her lips tightly together. "Guaranteed to chase off the evil pneumonia spirits."

Billie didn't need any magic potions. Once she was out of the lint-filled air, her sneezing would stop. But Martha didn't have to know that. "Thanks, Martha," she said.

Martha didn't reply. Her faded-green eyes were vacant as Billie hoisted her duffle and sleeping bag into position. At the door, Billie watched the old lady resume her wordless mumbling.

"Good-bye, Martha. And thanks again," she said.

In the crisp morning air outside the Quick Coin-Op, Billie heard Martha's wheezing voice as the door softly whumped shut. "Bye, now, Patsy. Stop again, darlin'."

SIX

The sun moved toward noon, strong and warm, but Billie's whole body shuddered and trembled. The trees and buildings on either side of the road blurred and danced like creatures in a Saturday morning cartoon, and she had to close one eye to bring the letters on the road sign together. Only a few more miles to Saliston, but Billie knew she couldn't go much farther. Even with daylight pointing out the earth's pockets and the rocks and roots ahead, she staggered and stumbled worse now than she had during all of the blind night-trekking.

Billie's nerves were as raw as her nose when she stopped for what seemed the fiftieth time to find a dry tissue. Determined not to let her runny nose slow her progress, she tore off hunks of tissue and wadded them into each nostril. She stopped for a moment and practiced breathing through her mouth. Over the soft, whistling squeaks coming from her chest, Billie heard an engine start up, then the rattling of metal across the road as a mud-splattered pickup truck rumbled out of the brush. The truck bed bounced crazily as the driver forced the truck up over a fallen branch and swerved onto the road, then squealed to a stop right beside Billie.

The man leaned out the open window. "Say, there, Sugar! Need a lift?"

Billie glanced quickly at him, then looked away. His face was young looking, but tufts of pure white hair stuck out from under a cowboy hat. "No thanks," Billie said. "I like the exercise." She began to walk on.

The truck followed alongside her. The man turned on the radio and began to sing. He leaned across the seat and draped his arm out the passenger window, pounding a rhythm against the side of the door. "You like country music?"

"It's okay," she said, forcing a smile while her heart and her mind raced. There was absolutely no traffic on this road, it seemed. Just her, and the rattly truck, and the driver with the strange hair and leering eyes, singing off-key. Billie's head ached and she couldn't think straight. Was this guy just trying to be friendly, or was he a weirdo, like the guy who killed Ma? What if he wouldn't leave? There was no one around to hear her if she screamed, and she couldn't run far on legs that felt like rubber bands.

Up ahead, off to the right, she thought she could see a dirt road winding through the tall grass. And farther into the weeds was something flat and green. A trailer! If the creep didn't disappear soon, she'd make a run for the trailer.

The man waved his arm in the air, nearly touching Billie's shoulder. "Not very friendly, are ya?"

Billie felt a sneeze coming. Ma said if you looked into bright light, you could make a sneeze happen really fast. She looked straight at the sun, then quickly turned her head toward the truck. The sneeze exploded from her, sending the tissue wads from her nostrils right into the window.

The man swore, and sent dirt swirling into Billie's face as he and the rattle-trap truck zoomed off.

"Good riddance!" Billie shouted after him. She stuffed more tissue wads into her nose and continued toward Saliston.

She hadn't gone more than a mile when the tickle in her throat turned into hard, racking coughs. Billie was forced to stop. She sat among the weeds, holding her sides together as the coughs threatened to pull her lungs right out into her hands. She tossed the Kleenex wads onto the ground, took short breaths through her nose, and waited for the flames to die down in her chest. Then the chills came, like waves splashing ice water over every inch of her body.

There had been only two cars on the road since the man in the truck drove away, and she hadn't seen any houses or other buildings along the way. She hated to turn around now that she knew where she was going, but she wasn't sure she could make it to Saliston without rest. Maybe the people in the green trailer, back down the road, could help her.

She staggered with the strain of lifting her pack to her shoulders and planned what she'd tell the people at the trailer. I'm working on a hiking badge for Girl Scouts? Yeah, that might sound okay. Or maybe I could just find Aunt Gloria's phone number and call her. The thought of actually talking to Aunt Gloria and ending the miles of walking helped Billie keep on.

Close up, the road leading to the trailer was little more than a dusty path, overgrown with weeds and moss. There were no fresh tire tracks, only dried-out double ruts beneath the weeds. Billie wasn't sure if she was relieved or disappointed that she probably wouldn't meet any people at this place.

She knocked on the door, listening to the rapping bounce around inside, and the silence that followed. She inched her way to the side of the trailer, glancing over her shoulder and peering around the scraggly trees which poked up, willy-nilly, amidst the tall grasses. Dried, brown vines clawed the sides of the rusty metal siding, and slime-wrapped minnow buckets littered the front stoop. In the back, old tires were stacked, like huge licorice Lifesavers, between two log piles.

Billie's teeth set to chattering once more as she pressed her nose against a window. Crusty dishes filled the tiny sink, and clothes were scattered everywhere. It was apparent that no one had been home here for a long time. She twisted the handle on the front door, but it wouldn't open. "This is an emergency," she said, pulling her knife from her duffle. She kept up a low-volume conversation with herself as she worked the knife around a window screen and pried it loose from the molding. "I've got pneumonia—Martha even knew it. No one could blame me for—"

She had to pound on the window before it would lift and she could climb inside. As she slid off the ledge, her legs began trembling and she fell to the floor. The trailer swayed slightly under her thudded landing, and over the sound of her pounding heart, she heard a noise in the kitchen closet. The door swung open.

She tried to scream, but only set off another coughing spell. By the time the racking, ripping in her chest had stopped, the mice had all scattered away.

"Maybe I'll have a heart attack before this stupid cough kills me," she said. She spread her sleeping bag on the narrow bed in the next room, hoping that whoever owned the trailer wouldn't decide to come back for a visit today. Smiling weakly, she imagined the Trailer Family returning. Little Trailer would shout, "Someone's sleeping in my bed!" and Billie would jump up and run out the door. The Trailer Family would stand on the steps, staring after her with mouths in perfect O-shapes, while Billie shouted over her shoulder, "And Billielocks never again wandered into strange houses without an invitation."

From the jar Martha had given her, she scooped out a large glob of yellowish slime. Billie turned her nose away as she reached her hand under her clothes and slathered the goop over her ribs and up her neck.

"This better work, Martha," she said, climbing into the sleeping bag. "Something that stinks *this* bad should be able to drive off the devil himself!"

She thought it would be hard to fall asleep with the blended odor of the poultice and the musty air surrounding her—and the thought of mice trying to share her covers. But as soon as she closed her eyes, her body went limp and she fell into a sound sleep.

Dream colors and images swirled together. Ma's face appeared: a head suspended in space with grape-purple skin. Ma smiled, then her purple skin began melting like gum left on a hot sidewalk. The purple Ma-face *drip-drip-dripped* into a puddle at the bottom of the dream. The puddle rippled as if stirred up. After the stirring, Ma's face was gone. In the glasslike surface, the wrinkled form of an old woman appeared, a twisted, pipe-cleaner body with a humped back. The old woman stared at Billie from the puddle, and smiled.

SEVEN

Friday, April 23. *There's an angel living at a laundromat in some little town in Minnesota. God sent her there so she could give me a bottle of gook that has holy healing powers. It stinks terrible, but I'm sure it was made in heaven. If I get a chance to talk to God, I'm going to suggest that He try a different scent. Chocolate or lilacs, maybe.*

I should be eight hours closer to Beacon City, but whatever kind of bug bit me, it got me good. I wasted half of the dark-time yesterday sleeping in that gross trailer. I'm not complaining, though. When I woke up, I was cured! No headache, no dizziness, no tractor parked on my chest. Cough's still hanging on, but I bought some expensive cough drops and some aspirin, too. Between me and Martha, those evil spirit germs don't stand a chance. But even a guttersnipe wouldn't smell this bad! I'll have to take another sink bath before I knock on Aunt Gloria's front door.

I tried to make up for lost time by keeping on

through the daylight this morning, but I nearly got picked up for skipping school. Well, not actually. But that nosy, gum-popping tall girl who took up walking beside me about five miles out of Saliston could have been trouble. I'm too close to Great Aunt Gloria now to take my chances. I took a side road, and left the girl wondering if I was escaping from jail or just a kid she'd never met, let out of school early so my mom could take me to the doctor.

That's how I found this wood shed. There's a house just over the hill, but no one'll see me sleeping between the rows of stacked logs. And when the sun goes down, I can hit the road again.

EIGHT

As Friday night's journey merged with Saturday's misty pink dawning, Billie could feel the promise of springtime coming closer. She shooed mice from the chewed-up front seat of a rust-speckled black sedan half-buried behind a collapsed barn. For the third time in two days, she studied the map Martha had given her. Now Wetherby was only about 20 miles away, and Beacon City looked to be about 60 miles beyond, off Interstate 50. She'd have to take an east-west highway tonight.

Billie folded the map and slithered beneath her quilt. She sucked on a cough drop and sighed. Another 90 miles, or more. Every muscle in her body throbbed from the cold and the wet and the miles of her six-day journey, and still there were probably three more days to walk before she'd meet Great Aunt Gloria. The sickness had been brief, but her energy was easily sapped, and her fingers and toes became more swollen with every mile she put behind her; Martha's poultice didn't work magic on those hurting places.

Maybe there would be a bus depot in Wetherby, and she could ride the rest of the way to Beacon City. There was still plenty of money left, and probably enough food in the duffle to last at least three more days, if she was careful. She shifted on the seat and closed her eyes. Things were turning out just fine, after all.

Billie awakened hot and groggy. She threw off the quilt and her parka and left the sun-baked car to wander around the ramshackle barn and stretch her legs. The sun was sinking slowly, but after she had something to eat, it would be safe to get back on the road. She took her time munching a handful of raisins, one at a time, and rationed out three crackers and a slice of jerky. The glass bottles of juice she'd bought in the morning had been heavier to carry than the box kind, but the screw-on cap allowed her to drink a little now, and save some for later. She washed down an aspirin and pulled out her pad.

Saturday, April 24. About one night's walk to Wetherby. Then I'm counting on a bus ride to Beacon City tomorrow. Make up the bed in the guest room, Great Aunt Gloria—here I come!

Tomorrow, Billie thought, as she walked

briskly to the highway. Tomorrow, tomorrow, tomorrow. She tromped through the marshy ditches and watched the sky turn dark. "Tomorrow!" she said aloud, giggling as she dashed across driveways and darted behind shrubs and trees. She was only *one day* from a home and a town and a relative she'd never have to leave. One more day, and she could wind up the plastic music box which she'd kept carefully tucked in the duffle. "Someplace" was just a little farther down the road! She hummed the "dandelions in a tear storm" tune as she walked.

After a few hours, the double-lane road narrowed to a single lane with almost no shoulder before the asphalt merged with the wild land. Old farm houses appeared in the distance now and then, but often there were long, lonely spaces of darkness between the dirt driveways that led up to the houses and barns. Only one house, a couple of miles back, had lights in the windows; Billie wasn't sure if the others she'd passed were even occupied. She kept up a lively pace, listening to the night sounds in the clumps of dark forest and blankets of fields beside the road. At first, the owl cries had sent a shiver along her spine, but soon she grew accustomed to their haunting calls. It was as if a battalion of hoot owls were watching with their shining gold eyes, *who-whoing* to guide her through the night.

It was close to ten o'clock when Billie heard rustling near the edge of the road. Whatever was in there sounded close. Too close. Goosebumps prickled on her arms, even under the warm parka, and she walked faster. But when the rustling stopped, so did Billie. She barely breathed. There was only a quiet, intermittent whimpering sound that seemed to silence the owls.

The whimpering didn't frighten Billie like the rustling had. This was a mournful sound, the cry of something small and harmless. She shined her flashlight through the narrow ribbon of trees, into the field. Patches of almost-melted snow matted down the field grass, making pouches inside the tall, unencumbered weeds. As the whimpering rose and faded, Billie moved the beam slowly across the field. She was about to be on her way again when she caught a glimpse of red-tinted snow. Blood! The crying thing was injured.

She crept through the trees, toe-heel, toe-heel, to soften the sound of her footsteps. "It's okay, little thing," she whispered. "I'm not going to hurt you." As she got closer to the bloody snow, the whimpering stopped. Billie continued to murmur, creeping now inch by inch toward the hollowed-out place which hid the animal from view. She parted the tall weeds and aimed the light through the opening.

Curled in the flattened grass was a puppy. Its clear, amber eyes stared into the beam and glistened with pain. A low growl rumbled in the animal's throat.

Billie set the flashlight on the ground and reached for the puppy. His growl turned to a snarl and his lip curled, exposing small, pointed teeth. Billie put her hands on her knees. "Easy, little guy," she said.

The growling escalated, and his eyes narrowed. She watched him turn to lick his left rear leg. He winced as his tongue worked the area methodically.

"Let's see what you've got there," Billie whispered, kneeling down and reaching toward the puppy's leg.

His head jerked up. He resumed his growling and teeth-baring.

"Okay, okay," Billie said, backing away. "You don't make friends easily, do you?"

She took her time digging through her pack, then began a hushed word-song. "It's okay . . . I won't hurt you . . ."

He lifted his head and sniffed the air, then settled his head on his paws as she advanced toward him. His growl softened. When she sprinkled orange peels near his muzzle, he cocked his head and the growling rumbled to a stop. He looked from Billie to the peels several times, then gobbled them up. Once again Billie knelt in front of the puppy, offering him more peelings in her outstretched palm. He kept his eyes trained on her as she spoke softly and slowly brought her hand closer to his mouth. Finally, he bent his head and lapped his tongue across her hand until the peels were gone.

"See?" she said, tentatively touching the top of his head. "I'm your friend." He ducked slightly, but didn't bare his teeth, so she placed her hand on the pale yellow hood of fur around his neck and stroked gently. Her hands warmed as she kept up the petting, and the puppy seemed to be less wary of her. She moved the light and her fingers down the length of his body. He cried out when she touched the moist wound near his left leg, and his head snapped around. He resumed growling, and Billie quickly took her hand away. "I'm sorry," she said, holding out a cracker to him. "Can we be buddies again?"

He took the cracker and tolerated her petting; soon his growl sounded more like the purring of a large cat. He stared at her with his gold marble eyes, unblinking. There was something in his eyes, something that was unlike any puppy she'd ever seen before. Something—*wild*.

This was no regular dog, Billie suddenly realized. A page of Mr. Fitzgerald's science encyclopedia flashed in her mind. She'd memorized the words while she put together her fourth-grade science report. *Coyote, small prairie wolf of North America. It has a tawny coat and a* . . . She remembered the picture she'd drawn with colored pencils.

She shined the light on the puppy's tail. Hardly noticeable, but there was a hint of black at the very tip of his bushy tail. Reaching back into her memory for the details contained in that science project convinced her. This was a baby coyote, and he couldn't be more than a few months old! Where were his parents? The other pups?

Billie glanced at her watch. It was nearly 11:30. She couldn't stay with the puppy much longer if she was going to reach Wetherby by morning. But if she continued on to Beacon City and left him in the field, would he die?

NINE

Billie poked her head out of the sleeping bag and peered at the brightening sky. She hadn't meant to sleep the entire night in the matted place beneath the newly leafing trees. The coyote whined. She lifted him from Ma's quilt into her lap.

"I just wanted to get you settled," she said, removing the T-shirt she'd pulled over his hind legs to keep him from worrying the wound. The coyote immediately set to licking the thin film of ointment from the fist-sized raw place.

"No, no, fella," Billie whispered. "That stuff will get rid of the infection."

The coyote's ears pricked up when Billie spoke, and he let out a weak growl before settling his head in her lap. Billie tore up a slice of cheese and crumbled crackers into her hand. The coyote tilted his head sideways, his ear resting on Billie's wrist, and licked her hand clean. She stuffed a slice of cheese and two crackers into her own mouth, then set the pup onto the ground.

"I've wasted enough time," she said, shaking dewy weeds from the sleeping bag and quilt.

The coyote's amber eyes watched as she tied their rolled-up beds, then knelt beside him. "I guess I can leave this for you," she said, spreading the shirt flat and lifting the pup onto it. "Probably better if you don't lay right on the cold ground for a while." She moved away from the circle of grass, from the pup's clear-eyed gaze. "See ya," she said.

The pup whined and raised his head. Billie dropped her gear and dug into the duffle pack. Squatting, she spread cheese and crackers on the ground in front of the pup, and sprinkled a handful of raisins on top. The coyote was motionless, except his eyes, which watched Billie's moving hands.

"Okay, that should hold you for a while," she said.

The coyote blinked, and put his head down on his front paws.

Billie backed away from him slowly, until she felt the asphalt road underneath her shoes. Then she turned toward Wetherby. A few more hours and she'd be across the border, only a day—two, at the most—away from Beacon City and Lovelien Lane Gifts and Aunt Gloria's guitar. Just a few more days, and she'd have a place to call home. *Someplace*—forever. She was so close now, she could practically see the big white house and the . . .

The pup's whimpering turned to a squeaky howl as he struggled to stand up. Billie sighed, and ran back to the forest nest she'd made for him.

She patted the T-shirt. "Lie down, fella. You just *gotta* stay here." She shook her shoulders to place the backpack more firmly. "And *I* just gotta go to Beacon City."

The pup settled back into his lying-down position. A brief flash across the golden eyes was the only hint of his pain.

Billie puffed up her cheeks and let the air explode out. "You'll heal by yourself. You're a wild animal, not some pampered poodle!" The melting dew began to soak into her sneakers. She retraced her steps, and watched the coyote from the road. He whined, and moved clumsily, finally getting onto all fours, only to collapse immediately. She could feel those gold marble eyes of his boring right into her heart as he stood and fell, stood and fell, stood and fell.

"I don't see this . . . I don't hear this . . ." she

muttered, looking away from the pathetic ball of wriggling yellow fur whining like a puppy in a pet store window. Over the plaintive whimpering came the sound of humming tires. Billie dashed off the shoulder and belly-flopped down beside the coyote. Headlights cut through the misty layer of fog above the road.

She raised up on one arm and glared at the coyote. "You made me forget about staying in the shadows during the day! All my hard work to get to Aunt Gloria's could've been for *nothing*, thanks to you!"

The pup twisted his head around to lick his wound. "Go ahead, lick all the medicine off. See if I care! If you don't die from the infection, maybe the ointment will poison you!" She crawled onto her knees. "Then I can get to Wetherby by tomorrow, anyway."

Billie ran to the road, scanning the shoulders on both sides, as far ahead as she could see before the road curved. No drainage pipes along *this* stretch of road. And no old trailers, or cars rusted to the ground. She looked back to where the coyote and her gear were clumped together. It seemed the coyote had moved closer to the stuff.

The sun was trying to bust through the misty sky, making yellow streaks on the high branches of the pines at the other edge of the field. Behind one of the trees, something glistened. She walked toward the sun-sparkles, and the coyote began to whimper.

"Give it a rest!" she hollered. "I'm not leaving." She scowled at him. "I *can't* leave now, in broad daylight." She kept her eye on the flashing bits of sunshine. "But I'm leaving at dusk, no matter how hard you whine and moan."

The thick rows of pine trees fenced in the far end of the field. Inside the first row, Billie cupped her hands around her eyes. As she moved into the shadows beneath the closely knit branches, the flickering light disappeared. She hiked through the underbrush to the other side of the woods.

"Omigosh," Billie sputtered, nearly tripping over some barbed-wire fencing imbedded in the grass. In the middle of the clearing, parts of the fence peered through the weeds and the log posts leaned at odd angles toward the ground.

Behind the fence posts, the earth dropped off into a concrete foundation, littered with leaves. An apple tree, snapped off from its trunk nearby, had collapsed into the basement. A ramp, Billie thought, scrambling down the tree trunk. She waded through the debris, uncovering a warped wooden coffee table and a rocker which had once been thickly padded. A pile of yellowed stuffing was scattered under the rocker, and there were bits of it amidst the leaves. She cleared stuffing and leaves from under the rails of the rocker and eased her bottom onto the saggy seat webbing. Finding a rocking rhythm she could hum with, Billie closed her eyes and tilted her face to the warming sunshine. When she ran out of tunes to hum, she heard the coyote's whimpers floating through the pines. She opened her eyes.

Was there anything she could do for the pup, or were wild animals better off left to their own survival instincts?

She surveyed the gray walls. Shadows from branches swaying above made dancing images on the weather-stained blocks. The coyote's wails grew louder. Maybe she'd already tampered with his instincts too much.

Billie's mind wandered to a time several years ago when she and Ma had been walking at night. Billie had seen a man lying behind a dumpster, rolling from side to side, hugging his arms around his belly. She tugged at Ma's hand. "Stop, Ma," she said. "That man's hurt—or sick."

"Probably good 'n' drunk," Ma replied, grabbing Billie's hand tightly and pulling her quickly along the sidewalk.

"But Ma," Billie insisted. "He needs help."

Ma kept her face straight ahead, not even glancing at the dumpster. When they had crossed the street and were well into the next block, Ma stopped. She grabbed Billie squarely by the shoulders, and fixed ice-blue eyes on Billie's face.

"You don't help just *anyone*," she said. "If you save another person's life, they're obligated to save *your* life."

Billie thought that was a nice idea. "What's terrible about that? I should think you'd want somebody to look out for us."

"God, no!" Ma stopped staring at Billie and began walking home. "I heard once about a man who saved a kid from drowning . . ."

Billie hurried to keep up with Ma's fast *click-click-click* on the sidewalk, and her words.

"That kid followed the guy around constantly," she continued, as if she were reading a storybook. "The kid said, 'I must not leave your side; I must be ready to save your life if tragedy threatens.' Drove the guy nuts."

Her heels stopped *click-clicking* and she looked down at Billie. "The man went stark-raving mad. I'm already half crazy with all your chattering; I surely don't want an old bum hanging around me, night and day."

Maybe that's why the coyote wanted to follow Billie—because she'd saved his life. She gazed up and down the cinder block wall, thinking how nice it would be to have a wild coyote looking out for her. Ma had tried to look out for Billie, but Ma had a hard enough time taking care of herself. And it hadn't seemed that Roger even tried to look out for Billie *or* Ma. If he had, maybe Ma wouldn't have died. He'd have taken her home that night, instead of getting mad at her and leaving her at the tavern. Then Ma wouldn't have stood alone in the dark, waiting for a taxi. She wouldn't have had her purse stolen and her throat slit. If Ma had had a coyote beside her, the coyote would have growled and snapped at the murderer and frightened him away.

The pup's whines came in short bursts, two or three at a time, then a brief moment of silence before he'd start up again. Billie stopped the rocker and got up. A wild coyote, looking after *her*; like having her own private guard dog. Nobody would bother her when she walked into Beacon City or her next new school, not with a coyote by her side. Aunt Gloria would take him in right along with Billie, like she adopted all the strays that wandered into her yard.

Billie smiled as she climbed out of the basement. She'd have to wait a few days, until the pup could walk better, but what was a few days when you'd have someone to protect you forever? And Great Aunt Gloria would be proud that Billie hadn't abandoned an injured animal.

As she reached the top of the wall, a bird flew into the basement, and began to work its beak on a thin, foil-backed insulation strip which hung from a wooden ledge. It tore off a hunk and glided toward the sunshine. Little sparks of light flickered from the foil. Billie straddled the apple tree and peered more closely at the wooden ledge.

"Omigosh!" she said, skittering up to the ground. "A door!" She remembered the glittering of sunshine on the food sign and the drainage pipe nearly a week ago. Was this sparkling just one more coincidence, or was God speaking again?

The coyote wailed to her.

"I'm coming," she hollered. Across the wide field she sprinted, yelling at the top of her lungs, "I'm coming, fella!"

He growled when she flopped down beside him, but once she put her hand to his head, he quieted.

"I guess I'm staying until your leg has healed," she said, wondering if the coyote was part of some holy plan she didn't understand—or if she was already going nuts.

The pup stretched his neck and put his head on her thighs.

"If we've got to stay together until you can save me from a tragedy, I suppose you should have a name." Billie fluffed the fur under his chin. "And if you're some sort of an omen, you better be a *good* one."

Billie squinted into the coyote's eyes; the gold marbles glowed. "Okay, I'm convinced; you're a good sign—*Omen!*"

She dumped raisins into her hand and shared them with Omen. "It's a ceremony," she told him. "Kind of a baptism, I guess."

Chewing quietly, solemnly, she heard tires again. The sun had melted the frost from the asphalt, and lifted the fog. She lay flat on the ground, praying that the trees and weeds would hide her. When the sloshing noise of the tires ceased, and only the calling of birds punctuated the silence, Billie sat up. She lifted Omen into her arms and moved as quickly as she could without jostling him.

"I found us a great hotel," she jabbered as she hurried through the pines. "It's not real fancy, but unless I'm as empty-headed as Roger says I am, the place behind the door will get us out of the wind and weather until you're better."

Omen looked up at Billie as if he understood every word she'd spoken. Now as she set him in the grass near the stone wall and returned for her gear, she hoped she wouldn't disappoint him. She hoped the door actually did go someplace safe and dry. She prayed with all of the prayers she had coming to her that this wouldn't be another one of those things that didn't turn out the way you planned them.

Billie pounded a rock against the rusted latch hinge until it let loose, then braced her foot against the concrete wall as she tugged at the heavy slatted door. It banged against the side of the foundation when it finally flew open.

Moldy, sour-onion air escaped from the dark cave, and glass crunched beneath her feet as she moved around the room. Dust-covered canning jars were randomly strewn on the deep wooden shelves which lined one wall, and burlap gunny sacks slumped against the opposite wall. Long, silvery webs reached in all directions from the bare light bulb in the middle of the room, making a low-hanging, fragile net above Billie's head. The entire room—floor, walls, ceiling—was concrete. It wasn't the Holiday Inn, but it would be dry, and very private.

Omen yelped, and Billie scrambled up to him.

"You're going to have to stop bawling. It doesn't appear there are any houses nearby, but we don't want to take any chances, okay?"

She scratched under his chin until the scared, wild look in his eyes disappeared, then set about building a sling.

"No elevators in this hotel," she told him as she knotted fishing line around each corner of Ma's quilt. After each knot was in place, she reeled off several yards of line before cutting it with her knife.

With Omen snuggled into the quilt, the four tough lengths of trilene tore into Billie's hands as she lowered him down into the basement. He whimpered during the entire, swing-jerking journey, and howled from the time Billie landed him gently on the leaf-covered floor until she scurried down beside him.

She looked into the old root cellar and sighed. It would be a job to turn that stinky room into a temporary home. None of the places where she and Ma had lived had been *this* bad.

It was close to evening when Billie swept the last of the dirt and broken glass into one corner of the basement, and hauled the burlap sacks of decayed fruits and vegetables into the woods. The young leaves on a maple branch made quick work of the cobwebs and dusty shelves, and it was a good broom, too. Now, if she could only think of a way to make a shovel, she could clean up Omen's bathroom-place behind the apple tree ramp. Until then, she covered the spot with leaves, and was grateful he wasn't scattering his business around the entire floor.

Billie carried Omen into the room behind the wooden door. "Welcome home," she said, settling into the quilt-draped rocker. The flashlight beam swung softly below the light bulb. Billie rocked Omen and looked around her little apartment. Her shoulders ached. Soon she'd fix their dinner and set it out on the wobbly coffee table, and try out the bunk she'd made on the lowest shelf. But first she'd listen to the music coming from the creaky rocker rungs, and the soft drumming of Omen's heart against her own.

TEN

During the daylight hours, Billie explored the land above her home. Whether some higher power had figured into finding the coyote and the secret room, Billie didn't know, but it couldn't have worked out more perfectly. Fields and forests continued to bump into each other far beyond the clearing which she now considered her yard. Across the highway were more acres of undisturbed grassy lands and forests. It was as if Omen had led her into a world people had not yet discovered.

When night came, Billie rocked Omen to sleep and nestled him on his T-shirt mattress beside her bed before she took up her pad. She wanted to capture Omen forever through her drawings, and words helped make the waiting-to-find-Gloria less frustrating. But she couldn't leave the flashlight shining too long; there were only two batteries left in her duffle. The night music of owl hoots and chirping crickets and distant coyote voices crept under the closed door and lulled Billie to sleep.

Sunday, April 25. For now, the secret room is our home. Omen has stopped crying and trying to pull off the gauze I taped over his wound. The cuts on my hand don't sting anymore.

Tuesday, April 27. It's clammy underground at night, and a little spooky. It doesn't help my heart stop thudding when Omen whimpers and wriggles every time some little animal skitters through the leaves on the other side of the door. Last night, a bat got into the room; nearly scared the wits outta me when Omen started hobbling around, snapping at the air in the pitch blackness. But he was quiet when I left him today, to go exploring.

There's a creek across the highway. The water tastes clean enough, if you don't think about straining the grit through your teeth while you're drinking, but I don't dare drink much of it. That Field Guide *book I bought in Compton says you gotta boil wild water so you don't get sick from the fish poop and other invisible stuff.*

Before I discovered the stream, I found a dented metal bowl. It's perfect for Omen's water, and the grit doesn't bother him a bit. I had to fill it three times before he let me quit running back to the creek.

Wednesday, April 28. There's mint growing near the creek—and some kind of plant that looks just like mint, but tastes like rotten vegetables smell. And there are fish in the creek! I cut off the top of a plastic milk jug I found in the weeds, and managed to scoop out a few fingerlings. The food supply is getting low, but I'm not so starving I'd eat those little fish raw, like Omen did. The mint leaves were okay, but not real filling. If Omen isn't able to walk pretty soon, I'll have to go to Wetherby for more food.

Billie tossed and turned in her sleeping bag throughout the night. Before first light Thursday, she was up, unzipping her sleeping bag and tossing it to the floor.

"I guess this place isn't as dry as it looks," she muttered as she threw off her damp night clothes and pulled dry ones from her duffle. Omen uncurled from his bed slowly and waited by the door.

"Yep, it's bathroom time, fella," Billie said, lifting Omen and carrying him up the tree trunk. She looked to the sky. "Good. The sun'll be shining today." She set Omen down and watched him limp into the brush. "I'll be back in a minute," she said, then scrambled back into the underground room to retrieve her sleeping bag.

Billie kept one eye on Omen as she spread the sleeping bag over the branch of a dead tree. "There!" She smiled. "This is now our official clothesline. The sunshine should take care of the dampness and the mildewy smell in this thing, and I'll have a dry bed tonight!"

She gathered Omen into her arms again. "So," she said, sliding her bottom carefully down the tree. "What would the Coyote King like to dine on this morning?" She sighed as she scanned the shelves above her bed. "Not much selection, I'm afraid."

That evening, Billie and Omen ate the last of the cheese and jerky; there were only six crackers left for tomorrow's breakfast, and a half-empty bottle of juice.

While she rocked Omen, Billie carefully removed gauze and adhesive from his hip. The wound looked less angry; it wasn't oozing anymore, and a scab was beginning to form. Billie put Omen on the floor and climbed onto her bunk.

"C'mere, Omen," she said.

Omen curled his tail around him and put his head on his paws.

"Come on, boy." She held out a cracker.

He got to his feet slowly. His gait was choppy, and his left leg dragged behind him as if it wasn't part of his body, but he made it all the way across the room.

"Good boy," Billie said, giving him his cracker reward.

But after he swallowed it, he sagged onto his bed and began licking his hip.

Billie smoothed ointment on the scab and covered it again with a dressing. "I'll have to go to Wetherby by myself tomorrow," she said.

She turned off the flashlight and snuggled into her sleeping bag. It smelled like sunshine. Her fingers found Omen's soft fur in the darkness below the shelf. It could take weeks for Omen to be able to make the long walk to Wetherby, she thought as she massaged his neck. *Weeks.* She simply couldn't wait that long for a real home, a place where she could let the tune out of the plastic music box.

"You've got me to sing *you* to sleep," she whispered down at the softly breathing lump, "but I want lullabies, too."

In the stillness, it came to her: if there was a bus to Beacon City from Wetherby, she could fetch Great Aunt Gloria by tomorrow afternoon, and they could come back to the secret room together to get Omen! He'd get better much more quickly in a real house, and Billie wouldn't have to wait any longer to learn Aunt Gloria's songs.

ELEVEN

In the morning, Billie filled Omen's water dish with creek water and set it on the coffee table.

"No, no, Omen." She pushed his head away from the dish. "This isn't your drinking dish right now; it's a sink." She dipped a T-shirt into the icy water and wrung it out. "I've got to get the guttersnipe smells off me today." Rubbing a bar of soap into a lather on the shirt, she grimaced as she worked the cold cloth over her body. Omen worked his tongue over his haunches. She laughed. "At least your bath is warm."

While she dressed, she hummed. "Wish me luck, ol' buddy," she said, still humming as she closed the slatted door and set food and water for Omen on the basement floor. Omen lapped the water without raising his head.

"Behave. And don't howl. Now that my cold's gone, I don't need you getting a sore throat!" She raced to the highway.

Though May was still a day away, the air felt like summer as Billie stepped off the bus at Beacon City. She rushed past the people milling around the depot with tour maps opened in front of them and headed for the Information Booth. The man behind the counter had his back to her, a telephone clasped tightly against his ear. He laced the cord through his fingers, then let it spring out from between them as he uh-hum'ed and nodded his head. Billie tapped her toe. Hurry *up*, she thought. It's already noon. Omen's going to think I'm never coming back.

The man hung up the phone and began shoving papers into a black file cabinet. Billie cleared her throat loudly. "Eh-hem."

"Yeah?" he said.

"I'm looking for Lovelien Gifts," Billie said. Her heart was pounding.

He smiled strangely at her. "Gift shops all down the block," the man said. "I suppose they've *all* got lovely gifts."

Billie snickered. "No, not *lovely* gifts," she said. "The store's name is *Lovelien*—Lane—Gifts."

"Never heard of it, kid." He turned back to the file cabinet.

Billie swallowed hard. "But it's here—in Beacon City—*some*place."

"Well, I never heard of it," the man said. He shrugged. "But I don't do much gift shopping. Try the phone book, over there." He pointed across the depot, to a row of phone booths.

Billie sat on the small stool inside the booth. She searched the small depot for one of God's glittery messages, but the windows were dingy and the sunshine didn't come in the door with the people. Billie pulled the book onto her lap and started with the White Pages. Gloria Lovelien wasn't listed. There were no Loveliens at all. She looked under *Gift Shops* and *Specialty Stores* in the Yellow Pages, but there was nothing that came even close to the three words she'd been waiting nearly two weeks to see. The phone book slipped from her lap and swung from its chain as Billie buried her face in her hands.

"Excuse me, honey. Do you need some help?"

The deep, kindly voice reached through Billie's snuffling. She wiped her nose across the back of her hand and looked at the gray-haired man in the striped suit.

He tilted his head toward her. "Can I help you?" he asked, his eyebrows raising slightly as he spoke.

"Probably not," Billie said, sliding off the

stool. She stood outside the phone booth, staring down at her shoes.

"I'm the unofficial mayor of Beacon City," he said. "Been here nearly as long as this depot." He smiled broadly. "Ask me anything, dear. What's the worst that could happen?"

My heart will bust apart, Billie thought. But she said, "Okay. Have you ever heard of Lovelien Lane Gifts?"

"My stars!" he whooped. "Haven't heard that one in a good long time."

Billie moved closer to the man. "You mean you know the store?" She could feel her blood pumping again.

"Why, sure," he said. "My wife spent a small fortune on Gloria Lovelien's imported do-dads."

"Where is it?" Billie asked. "The store— where—"

"It *isn't*," the handsome gentleman answered. "Miss Lovelien closed the shop six, seven years ago."

Billie looked away, frantically searching for a glimmer of sunshine somewhere—anywhere. "And the owner—Miss Lovelien? Where is she?"

The man laughed. "Oh, my darlin', that's anyone's guess. England . . . Germany . . . France? Maybe Africa, to save the tigers . . . or

Antarctica, to save whales or penguins or whatever else might need saving." He smiled down at Billie. "Gloria Lovelien was—*different*. But she had a big heart."

Great, Billie thought. Just great. Gloria's big heart wasn't going to do Billie any good, beating somewhere in Africa or France.

The man shifted his briefcase from one hand to the other. "If you're looking for a special gift," he said, "my wife tells me The Glass Shelf, on Dotter Street, has exquisite things." The man pushed up his jacket sleeve and looked at his watch.

"Thanks," she replied, ". . . for your help." She watched him walk out the depot door. Not even one of his gray hairs glistened in the sunlight. She took out her wallet and returned to the ticket counter. "One way, to Wetherby," she said.

Billie wandered the streets outside the bus station, working hard to push the Great Aunt Gloria dream back into the place in her mind it had once been hidden. She tried to make the "dandelions in a tear storm" tune stop humming inside her head, but like an annoying mosquito, the humming just got louder. She tried to erase the sketch in her mind of a white house and a green lawn, but it stayed there as if it had been glued into place. And underneath the picture she could imagine a pink eraser moving over the word Someplace.

Back at the secret room, Omen was waiting; it was something. She couldn't live there forever, that was certain. She'd never survive without heat in the winter. But for now, it would do.

She wheeled a cart around the Beacon City Market. Earlier in the day, her wallet seemed stuffed with money, but now she knew she'd have to shop smart. There was no telling how long it would take to come up with a new dream to replace the Aunt Gloria one. She tried to remember the food chart Miss Mikler hung in the third-grade classroom. Nuts and fruit were both healthy, but fruit was cheaper. She put the jar of peanuts back on the shelf, and dropped a bag of apples into the cart. She added carrots and potatoes. They'd taste okay raw, and they wouldn't spoil quickly, especially in a root cellar room.

It was 1:15. She'd have to hurry if she was going to make the two o'clock bus back to Wetherby. She lingered in the housewares aisle, wishing she could afford a pot or a skillet. She imagined warm plates of scrambled eggs for breakfast and fried fish for dinner—and clean water. When she'd first thought about escaping from Roger, she'd read lots of books to help her prepare if the opportunity ever came. She needed to remember everything now.

To purify the water, she'd need something to boil it in. She lifted a small frying pan from the shelf. Five dollars for one puny pan? She put it back. The discount store she'd passed on her way from the depot would surely have cheaper prices.

Counting on bargains down the street, she tossed powdered milk, soup, cereal, and eggs into the cart with peanut butter, baked beans, and crackers. At the check-out, she piled juice, cheese, and canned vegetables onto the conveyor belt. She held back a package of hamburger meat, considering whether she should treat Omen and herself to a juicy burger.

"You buying that meat, or not?" the cashier said.

"I don't know," Billie answered. "How much is it so far?"

The lady clicked her tongue and sighed, but she subtotaled Billie's groceries anyway. "$17.35."

Billie grinned. "Yeah," she said. "Add it in."

At the discount store, she picked out a small

aluminum frying pan and a spatula, then sifted through a laundry basket heaped with mismatched plastic plates and silverware. The taped-on sign offered Billie a bargain she couldn't refuse: YOUR PICK, 25-CENTS. As the pimply-faced boy tallied the prices, Billie added a box of matches to the pile. If she was going to cook, she'd need a fire, and she wasn't sure how to do that by banging rocks together. "Oh! These too," she said, remembering flashlight batteries and dish soap.

The boy seemed to take forever adding and re-adding. "You a camper?" he asked.

"Yeah," Billie said. *Permanently, probably.*

"Well, you came to the right place for supplies." He snorted. "Mostly warehouse rejects, but you can't beat the prices."

As the bus bumped along the road, stopping frequently at remote gas stations or cafes to let people off or pick up others, Billie couldn't help grinning. Just over $25.00, and she could barely carry all of the stuff she'd bought. And she still had the *Field Guide* book in her duffle, to help her find free food. Maybe she and Omen would do okay on their own, after all. As the bus traveled toward Wetherby, Billie counted in her head. Four months, at least, to build a new dream. Surely she'd know what to do by the time September rolled around.

At the next stop, Billie thought of the eight-mile hike back to Omen, weighted down with the bags. She walked to the front of the bus. "Is Wetherby your last stop?" she asked the driver.

"Nope. Saliston's the end of the line."

Saliston? Billie couldn't believe her ears. She could have been on a bus to Beacon City days ago—before she ever even stumbled onto Omen and the underground room. She shrugged. "And what good would that have done?" she mumbled. "You wouldn't have had anywhere to go to now."

"You say somethin', Miss?" The driver scrutinized her from the rearview mirror.

Billie cleared her throat. It was too much to hope for, but still she asked, "Are you taking Interstate 50?"

"Yep." He pulled the door shut.

Billie sat in the seat behind him. "Do you suppose it'd be okay if I rode a little farther than Wetherby?"

"You paid to go to Wetherby, kid. How much farther you want to go?"

"About eight miles, is all. And I could pay more, if you want."

He glanced over his shoulder. "Sure, why not? Save your folks a trip to town, eh?"

"Yeah, right." Billie had to suck back the *whoopee!* that wanted to burst right out of her.

"You just let me know when we get near your house, okay? No charge."

"Okay! And thanks."

Billie could hardly sit still, watching out the window for a good spot to get off the bus. She waited until they'd passed a farm house, set far back from the road, then took her time gathering her bags and making her way to the front. "We passed it," she said. "Just a little ways back."

"Nearly a mile back, as I recall," the driver said as he ground the gears to a stop. "You've got a little hike ahead of you, I'm afraid."

Black exhaust clouds puffed into the air as the bus took off. The driver had deposited her less than a mile, as far as she could guess, from the stand of trees and the field where she'd first happened upon Omen. Her bags *bump-twacked* around her as she hurried toward the secret room.

Before she reached the clearing, she heard howling in the distance, far beyond the foundation. Then a solo voice, distinctly Omen's.

"Ar-ar-ar-ooo . . ." His voice echoed up from the cinder block walls.

She laughed and sang back, "Ar-r-r-ooo."

"Ar-ar-ar-ooo . . . Ar-ar-ar-ooo . . ." he answered.

Billie kept up her howling as she dropped the bags beside the apple tree ramp and slid-stepped down into the basement.

Omen had chewed off the bandage, but he struggled to his feet and met her at the bottom of the tree.

She ruffled his fur and scratched his ears. "Did you think I'd leave you here?" she said. She picked him up and carried him into their room. "Wait here; I've got a surprise for you. A whole bunch of surprises!"

He didn't wait. He limped over to the tree-steps and followed her with his eyes as she scrambled up and down the tree three times to get all of the bags into the room behind the door. She spread peanut butter thickly on a cracker, and offered it to Omen. His tail swished as he pulled the cracker between his lips and lolled his tongue against the roof of his mouth.

Billie laughed. "Good, huh? And that's just a start." She held the package of ground beef under his nose. "The main course tonight is Billie-style Burgers!"

She gathered dried twigs and branches and

built a teepee fire in the corner of the foundation. Omen licked his lips as the cooking aromas steamed from the pan. Billie mimicked him. "Yeah, I'm drooling, too," she said.

They sat on the floor by the wobbly table for a long time, licking every bit of juice from their plates. "Here," Billie said, giving him another cracker with peanut butter. "Have your dessert while I get water."

Racing against the gathering dusk, Billie ran to the creek and back with the plastic jug. Far off, the coyotes were tuning up for their night singing. She washed the pan and set it on the hot coals, wondering if Omen heard the coyotes. If he did, did he know that he was one of them?

The first drops of creek water sizzled as Billie filled the pan. "I'll just make a little clean water tonight," she said as Omen watched from the doorway. "Tomorrow we'll boil up a ton of creek water and store it in some of those old canning jars." She stirred milk powder into the water, mashing the floating globs against the side of the pan until the milk cooled, then poured some for Omen and herself.

"I'm stuffed," Billie said as she put the groceries on the shelves above her bed and began to think about sleeping. If she and Omen were going to make this home permanent, she had lots of work to do tomorrow.

Omen whimpered softly as she rocked him. "I know, buddy," she whispered. "You thought you'd be sleeping on a soft rug in Aunt Gloria's big ol' house tonight. And I thought Great Aunt Gloria would be strumming songs for me." She pulled Omen against her chest, and he nuzzled his nose into her neck. When she leaned her head on his, he raised up and licked the salt off her cheeks. She held him tightly, until the lump rising in her throat dissolved.

"Time for bed, puppy," she said, laying him beside her bunk.

She reached around him, and dragged her duffle from under the shelf. She pulled a sweater-wrapped lump from inside. Carefully, she uncovered the plastic music box with the dancing couple on top, and set it on the shelf in front of the groceries.

"Perhaps this is the Someplace Ma sang about, Omen," she said. "When we know for sure, I'll let you hear the music."

Before she shut off the flashlight she propped her pad in her lap.

Friday, April 30. This place doesn't have black shutters; it doesn't even have windows. But

it's all mine—and Omen's—and nobody will
ever find us. Now all I have to do is figure out
where we'll go when the summer ends. And how
to survive with only $168.92.

TWELVE

May awakened slowly, stepping as carefully into its new life as Billie and Omen did. Once it started, it seemed to race forward, splashing the fields and forest with wildflower-color. Billie and Omen matched May's pace, first tiptoeing, then running in the sunshine and fragrant breezes as Billie became certain of their safety, and Omen's wounds healed.

In the daytime, Billie and Omen studied the woods and the creek, checking anything which looked edible against the pictures in the *Field Guide*. Early each morning, Billie shrugged into her backpack and scrambled up the tree, then crouched at the top of the foundation, coaxing Omen to try the ramp on his own. Finally, after two weeks, Omen didn't back away from the tree trunk as soon as his paws touched it, and lie down whimpering; he kept his eyes on the beef jerky Billie held out to him and teeter-tottered all the way to the top.

"All *right*! You did it without any help this time." She kissed the top of his head. "Keep practicing, and maybe I can find you a job with a circus!"

Omen was close on Billie's heels as she ran across the field, shouting, "Folks! You are about to witness the most amazing, most daring tree trunk climb in all of history. In the center ring, from the depths of the forests, is Omen the Awesome, the climbing coyote!" Omen began to howl.

"Perfect timing!" Billie said. "Your singing will steal the show!" She stopped near the creek and opened the *Incredible Edibles* book. "But until we can perfect your act, we can't count on your salary to feed us, and we can't spend all of our money on burgers."

Omen followed as Billie moved her fingers through the tall grasses, uncovering wintergreen berries and small, black beetles. The wintergreen berries were plentiful and easy to collect. "The book tells how to make jelly from these berries," she called to Omen as he nosed along the creek, catching his own frog-snacks.

Until now, Billie had purposely skipped the page of Beetle Recipes in the book, but mid-May didn't offer much selection in wild edibles, and grocery shopping dwindled her funds too quickly.

"Beetle Cake sounds about as appetizing as those frogs you're slurping down," she said, "but I guess it's time to develop a taste for something new." Billie remembered reading a book once about a kid who ate worms. Beetles didn't sound nearly as disgusting as worms. She guessed it was the price she'd have to pay for not yet figuring out a plan beyond the secret room.

Free food, she reminded herself as she reached to pluck a beetle from the grass. It quickly scurried away. *"Free food, free food, free . . ."* She set the words to music, singing them to block out the thought that later, her stomach would be full of once-squirmy, thin legs. "Gotcha!" she said, cupping her palms around the first beetle. It looked small on top of the berries in the pack. She sighed. The Beetle Cake recipe didn't say how many beetles make a half-cup, but she guessed she'd be beetle-picking a long time.

The sun was high when she stood and rubbed the cramped places from her back and legs.

"Omen!" she called, anxious now to get back to the room and put the recipe to the test. If she ever did find someplace else to live, the kids there would really think she was something to be able to eat bugs. The worm-eating kid was a hero by the time the story ended. "C'mon, Omen!" she shouted, jerking the backpack from the grass. "I'm starving!"

Billie listened for his rustling among the weeds, but there were no sounds. Even the wind was still. She threw the pack down. "Great! I've been picking bugs all morning, and now I have to go on a coyote search! Where *are* you, Omen?" She tromped down to the creek, nearly running into him at the edge of the water. He was frozen still; he didn't even look up when she stood right beside him.

"What is it?" she asked, following his stare. "Oh, wow!" she said. "Perch! That beats bug-biscuits for lunch any day! I don't have to rush into this hero stuff, I guess."

Omen remained motionless, his tail tucked tightly behind him and his eyes riveted on the fish.

"If only I had a fishing pole—or a net . . ." She quickly pulled off her T-shirt and knotted each sleeve and the neck opening to close off the holes. "You stay right there, Omen," she said, moving along the bank, upstream.

"Easy, easy," she whispered, as much to herself as to Omen while she removed her shoes and stepped into the icy water. She made her way back to Omen, the shirt bubbling out beside her as she dragged it through the stream. Moving in slow-motion, deliberately lifting each foot one toe at a time from the pebbles and muck beneath her, she thought surely she'd lose her balance. She was only a few yards from Omen when he put one paw into the water and sent the perch swimming toward her. Blindly, Billie whooshed the shirt forward and arched it to the surface.

"We got one!" she screamed. "We got one!" As she watched the flopping and flipping going on inside the shirt, Omen splashed toward her. "Good work!" she said. "Good—"

Omen jumped and pulled the shirt from Billie's grasp. The fish splashed into the creek as the shirt dangled from Omen's teeth.

"You Bozo!" Billie said, shaking her head. "Now I have to eat beetles for lunch!"

Mixed with flour and sugar and eggs, the fried beetles gave the little cakes a nutty flavor, just as the book had claimed. Billie just tried not to listen when the nutty flavor crunched against her teeth, reminding her of the beetles' hard shells. "Not as gross as worms, but I wouldn't want a steady diet of bugs," she told Omen as she boiled water to wash their dishes. Billie laughed. "Next time, you can't get so excited if we catch a fish. But we *did* catch one. And it'll be a lot easier after I make us a real fishing pole."

She was glad that the man who'd written the *Field Guide* had included the "Improvised Survival Tools" chapter at the end of the book. That night, after letting Omen out for his run, Billie made a soft seat in the middle of the root cellar with a pile of dirty clothes, and set to whittling notches in the end of a birch branch. She unwound several yards of fishing line, knotting it tightly in the grooves at the end of the branch exactly as the directions showed. She tied a hook on the other end, then pulled the line tight all the way to the handle-end, coiled the excess around the twig stubs on each side, and carefully locked the hook into the coiled line.

"All right! With a worm wiggling at the end of this beauty, we're guaranteed some fish dinners!" She stood the pole against the wall.

Outside, she tamped down the last embers of the fire, then hollered for Omen. "C'mon," she muttered on her way to the thicket where she'd dug her latrine. Far off, she heard a chorus of wild yipping. Her heart seemed to stop pumping for a moment, but before she could carry her worries to a real thudding place, Omen crashed through the brush and beat her down to the cellar.

"Wash day tomorrow," she said, shoving the

dirty clothes into a corner. "And then maybe I should go exploring to find out how far the unpeopled space goes."

Omen's only answer was a soft snore.

THIRTEEN

Beyond the clearing, the forest was thick and dark. Billie tied strips of cloth around tree branches as she moved deeper into the woods, wishing she'd brought Omen along. He'd be able to find his way back home without any help at all. But if she *did* come upon anyone, she'd be better able to hide without him.

She ducked low branches and stepped over thick vines until the woods thinned and the young grass was like a soft carpet under her feet. She shielded her eyes. Only a few feet beyond, barely visible in the new ground growth, was a path winding through the trees. A path made by animals—or people?

She moved on, glancing constantly from side to side and up ahead until her eyes felt as if they'd unscrew right out of the sockets. Suddenly her legs locked up, and she dropped behind a wall of boulders. A garden! Long, neat rows, lined on either side with straw and leaf mulch, appeared like a mirage, but the scent of turned soil and manure told Billie this was not her imagination. And a tended garden meant . . . she and Omen hadn't been as alone in the woods as she'd thought.

Billie poked her head above the rocks. Past the garden, to the right, was a field that seemed to run off into forever. To the left, not far from the garden, was an old, white house, tucked behind a sparse grove of fruit trees. And between the garden and the orchard were animals poking up from the lawn like they'd been frozen in place. Sculptures! Billie had to squint to see the rabbits and squirrels nestled in the grass. The deer were life-sized, too, and so real-looking she expected them to flick their white tails and bolt off if she breathed too loudly.

Curtains fluttered behind an open window at one end of the porch, and vines wound around the porch posts—deep green leaf-ribbons circling huge purple flowers. Metal butterflies fluttered against the porch swing chains, sending chime sounds straight into Billie's thumping heart. She ducked back behind the rocks.

Her mind raced as fast as her heart: Whoever the gardener is, he knows what he's doing. Soon vegetables will be popping up as plain as the sculptures—a Produce Department in the woods! Her thinking did a U-turn: Anyone who made such perfect rows would keep a close eye on the whole growing process. And the sculptures . . . they were probably valuable. If she was going to shop here, she'd have to be very careful.

She peered again at the house. Was the wind moving the curtains, or was someone holding them aside, looking out into the backyard? Billie didn't wait to find out.

Omen's tail was wagging when she burst through the door of the secret room, but she didn't stop to scratch his ears or rub under his chin. "Wait! I've got to figure out—" She scribbled furiously in her sketch book.

It took maybe forty-five minutes—tops—to get to the house with the garden. When I was running from Roger, I could make about thirteen miles a night. And that was straight walking—no gnarly branches trying to claw out my eyes and rip my hair out by the roots. That house can't be more than a mile from here—probably less. What if the guy who lives there is some nature nut who likes to hike in the forest?

Billie dropped her pencil. "My markers!" She jumped up and slammed the door in Omen's face, hurriedly retracing her steps to the rocks and collecting the cloth strips as if this were an Olympic relay event and her life depended on winning.

"We'll have to be careful with our fires," she told Omen as she stirred potatoes and onions for dinner. She divided the vegetables between them, filled the pot with water and set it on the fire. "No more hot meals, except after dark."

Omen's head was buried in his bowl, his tongue lapping the sides. Billie doused the fire and piled the dishes into Omen's empty bowl, then poured hot water and dish soap on top. "Dish washing only after dinner—and clothes washing, too. And I'd better rig a drying line in the basement; can't hang our stuff from a tree in plain view anymore."

Omen whined near the tree ramp.

"Okay, we'll go to the creek in a minute." She swished a cloth over the dishes hurriedly and set them on a towel to drain.

Like always, Omen slurped frogs and minnows for his bedtime snack, but Billie didn't drag sticks through the water, splashing and whooping as she usually did. Tonight she felt invisible ears listening in the darkness, and knew she'd have to spend more time in the underground room. She considered how she might ward off the boredom that was sure to set in.

"The daytime adventures were fun while they lasted," she mumbled as she worked her fingers along the creek bottom, searching for flat, white rocks. "But that gardener guy is too close for comfort." Once Ma told her that Indians and pioneers painted grand pictures on stones, with only berries and leaves for paint. Maybe she could try that. Her sketch pad was beginning to fill up. Too many words with the pictures. She filled her pockets with rocks and scrambled along the bank to gather the bright blue and red berries the *Field Guide* warned were poisonous. That wouldn't be a problem; she didn't plan to *eat* her rock paintings.

Under the swinging light, Billie squashed berries and mashed leaves. Omen settled on his T-shirt bed.

"You're so lazy," she said as she sharpened and frayed the end of a willow stick.

Omen blinked and grinned without raising his head from his paws.

Billie dipped the stick into the leaf mush, then carefully drew stems and leaves onto the biggest, flattest, whitest stone she'd collected. She made oval shapes from blue berry-paint until the thick color raised up like flower petals.

"Wow! It worked!"

Omen ambled over to sniff the painted stone.

Billie held it over her head. "Be careful! Don't gop it up with your wet nose." She brought it back down, cradling it in her open palm. "I'll bet somebody would pay fifty cents—maybe more—for an original rock painting." She grabbed the painting stick and printed her initials below the flower. "When you're an artist, you have to sign your work, so people know it's important art." She wondered if the gardener's sculptures had initials carved in them somewhere.

Omen nudged her knee, then returned to his bed. "Okay, I'll turn out the light after I paint one more rock. Should I make geometric designs on the next one, or try to paint a picture of the creek?"

Omen's eyes were closed, his sides gently moving in and out in sleep-breathing when Billie finally climbed onto her bunk. With someone living so close to the secret room, she might have to move out before summer ended. She sighed and shut her eyes. In her dreams, there were always solutions to problems . . .

She and Omen walk along straw paths, gathering tomatoes and cucumbers and peppers until the brown grocery sack she carries is filled. A thin, white-haired man bolts from behind a rock pile, waving a sharp-tined tiller at her. His face is red, puffy, and he's screaming, but she can't hear his words. Animal sculptures come alive, leaping behind the man. A wolf bares his teeth and charges toward her. Men in uniforms crash through a grove of apple trees, tossing huge nets over Omen and clamping metal cuffs around her wrists . . .

Billie tossed the sweaty covers aside. Her hand fanned the space under the bed until she felt Omen's fur on her fingers. He picked his head up and nuzzled her hand.

"It's okay, boy. Go back to sleep. I just had a bad dream, that's all." She settled back on the bunk, determined to find a better dream than the one which had awakened her. No one would take Omen away from her, no matter what! Within seconds of closing her eyes, the uniformed men reappeared in the new dream . . .

The men turn the grocery bag upside down, and painted rocks tumble out. She and Omen walk away, past the red-faced man, into a dimly lit station. She sits beside a phone booth, behind a green metal card table heaped with painted rocks and birch bark etchings, the sounds of arriving and departing buses rumbling in her ears. Omen sits beside the table, as still as a stuffed animal. People gather to snap photos of the coyote and examine price tags on the art objects. They choose among the rocks and bark etchings, and toss quarters and dollars into the dented metal bowl beside Omen until it overflows . . .

FOURTEEN

Now that Billie knew about the house and the garden, she needed to know who lived there, what their daily schedule was; then she could plan her own schedule, and Omen's, and the secret room could still be her Someplace a little while longer.

The next three trips to the rock hiding place gave Billie no new information. The window was still open, and sometimes the curtains fluttered when Billie thought the air was still, but no one came out of the house, even though she waited behind the rocks for nearly two hours each day. Perhaps the gardener guy was a hermit. That would be very convenient, Billie thought.

The garden was further along than she'd realized. Most of the rows were only humped-up lines of rich soil, but light-green leaves fanned out at one end of the garden, and darker leaves made circle-groups along the last row inside the fence which separated the garden from the field. Bright green vines climbed metal stakes, their leaves reaching toward the sun. The plants weren't really mature, but they were close. One bright night soon, she'd come back to check if anything was ripe enough for picking.

Evening after evening, Billie watched the sky. Finally the night she'd been waiting for arrived. The moon hung like a round lantern suspended in darkness, lighting up the earth below. Near midnight, she gave Omen his nightly run, then grabbed her backpack and flashlight. "I'm going shopping," she said, closing him in the secret room.

The moonlight painted the garden a soft golden color. Even at this late hour, the porch window and two windows on the second floor were lit up. Billie watched for people-shadows inside, but nothing disturbed the light. She hoped everyone was reading or watching T.V. as she crawled on her hands and knees to the wire fence. It was thin, wobbly, more like window screen than fencing. Since it lined only the back of the garden, Billie wondered why it was there at all. It didn't keep any critters from snacking; there were deer tracks all through the dirt. Were they crossing the garden to see the clay animals?

She continued crawling, not wanting her visit

to be as obvious as the deer's. Carefully she lifted her hands and knees along the straw-strewn places to the dark-leaved plants. Spinach! She ripped several leaves and stuffed them into her mouth, remembering the first time she'd eaten raw spinach.

"It's delicious," Ma said as she washed the big, curly leaves and laid them on paper towels. "Full of vitamins—and great in salads."

Billie took the leaf Ma handed to her and studied it. "Spinach tastes like seaweed," she said.

"Not *raw* spinach," Ma replied.

Billie nibbled on the end of the leaf, pretending she was a rabbit. "It tastes like grass," she told Ma, finishing it. "Like grass . . ." She reached for another piece. ". . . but better."

Billie gently pulled leaves from each plant along the row and put them in her backpack. She glanced at the house before working her way to the other side of the garden, certain now that the lighter-green plants were lettuce. Again she took only a little from each plant. Ma said if you were careful when you harvested, the plants would reward you and produce even better.

At the end of the lettuce row were taller, feathery leaves. Carrots? She yanked, and the dirt let loose of the whole plant. Radishes! It was hard to resist pulling up more, but she especially wanted these to keep growing. She thought of the windowsill radish garden she and Ma planted the summer after first grade. Radishes grew fast; in a few weeks, they'd be as big as plums. And the big ones would be extra spicy, stinging her tongue, just the way she loved them best. She put the one round treasure with the lettuce and spinach. That's enough for one night's work, she decided.

Nearing the fence, the silent night suddenly filled with music—strange, haunting sounds like a mixture of whistle notes and bird songs floating out to the garden from the house. Billie sprawled flat into the dirt and turned her eyes slowly to the porch without lifting her head.

A large woman sat in the porch swing, her dark hair flowing like a shawl over her shoulders. As her fingers danced upon the long wooden instrument she had pressed to her lips, she turned her head toward the garden and sent snake-charmer tunes into the air. Billie wondered if the woman could see between the apple trees into the garden. Did she know Billie was spread like a rug in the dirt, or was she only dreaming, not seeing anything? Billie pillowed her head on the earth, squeezing her eyes shut and holding her breath. If the woman knew someone was there, she'd stop playing the odd flute soon.

But the music continued without a pause. Billie stopped counting seconds and minutes and relaxed as the music worked its way into the empty places inside her. She stayed flat in the garden even after the trilling music stopped and the porch door slammed shut. When all but one upstairs window darkened, she crawled out of the garden. All the way home, the moon seemed to be winking down at her, as if it had been enchanted tonight, too.

FIFTEEN

Saturday, May 29. *I've been checking the house by the rocks every day and every night, but I never see anyone except the dark-haired lady. I guess the gardener isn't a guy, after all. The first time she came outside in the daylight, I thought I'd keel over. She glanced toward the rocks and began to weed the garden and sing. Her singing is a little like her flute music, warbly and strange, but pleasant and soothing, like the murmurings of people from other lands.*

Another time, I heard her singing through the open window. One minute, she was resting her chin on the window ledge, staring straight across the field as if she were seeing things that weren't there, and the next minute, she started singing, then moved away from the window. Later, chocolate scents rushed out the window, and I imagined her taking brownies or cookies from the oven. I wondered if she was lonely, living in that big house all by herself. I thought about knocking on the red door, telling her that her brownies smelled wonderful and would she like help eating them, but, of course, I couldn't do that. So I just tucked the chocolate smells in my memory, and made spinach salad and beetle cakes for dinner.

Three nights ago, I went back to check on the radishes. And hear the night music. The big lady was already on the porch playing her flute when I got to the rocks. After she stopped playing, she leaned on the railing for a long time. "Is someone out there?" she called. Her voice wasn't angry or scared, like mine would be if I thought somebody was lurking in my backyard, waiting to steal my stuff. But still, my heart started pounding like crazy and I waited until all the lights went off in the house before I snuck into her garden. And I was real careful. I took only a little bit of the lettuce and spinach, and I tried to tear the leaves sort of ragged-like, so she'd think a rabbit stole 'em. I yanked the radishes up with my teeth, and scratched around the row with my fingernails. That's how a raccoon would do it, I think.

Her strawberries are getting big and red; they're going to be lots better than the teeny wild ones near here. But I think I'd better be extra careful if I go back again soon. It would be awful if she caught me before I got a taste of those strawberries.

It's time to go to Wetherby again, anyway. I

can't get everything I need from nature and that lady's garden, no matter what.

Twice now, Omen ran off and stayed gone all night. Each time, I was worried that he'd found the wild coyotes, but he was back pawing at the door by sun-up. He brought me a rabbit the first time, and a squirrel the next. Took a long time to cut away the fur and guts and stuff, but it tasted great, just like the Field Guide *said.*

I never hear the far-off coyotes howling in the day. I wonder if the garden lady plays her flute only at night, too?

SIXTEEN

It was mid-June when Billie thought about winding up the music box and letting Omen hear the song. She was gathering roots for dinner as Omen sniffed around a blackberry thicket. "How about a rabbit to go with these vegetables?" she called, and suddenly she wondered what Ma would think about the food Billie was eating these days. She could imagine Ma scolding, "You call this *Someplace*? Cookin' up critters that have been killed by a wild dog? Bugs in your biscuits? Stealin' from your neighbor's garden?" Ma's idea of Someplace hadn't been anything like the Someplace Billie had come to love.

Back in the foundation outside the underground room, Billie readied her cooking fire, then sliced scraped roots into boiling water. As the turnip-tart aroma rose from the pot, Billie opened a jar of applesauce and cleaned the first strawberries from the flute lady's garden. Her mouth watered. Omen appeared at the top of the wall with a squirrel clamped tight in his teeth.

"It's about time you got your butt in gear! I was beginning to think we'd never eat meat again."

She looked up into the darkening sky. "Well, Ma," she said. "I guess everyone's *Someplace* is different."

Before bed, Billie took the music box from the shelf and held it out to Omen. "Tomorrow it'll be exactly two months since I took off to find someplace right for me. I'll let the song out of the music box in the morning!"

It was earlier than usual when Omen's pacing and whining in front of the door brought Billie from her covers.

"It's barely morning. What's your problem?" She groaned and slid off her bunk. Omen nudged Billie's leg with his paw, then sat by the door, working his whimper into a serious howl.

"Okay, okay." She reached for the door latch. "But don't stay out there too long, y'hear?"

Dawn squeezed through the creaking-open door, and with the pink light, sounds crowded into the little room—sounds that made Billie's skin turn clammy. She grabbed the fur behind Omen's neck and pulled up hard. "Wait!"

Omen whimpered frantically, tugging under

Billie's grip. She slammed the door and sank to the floor. "Bulldozers," she said, wrapping her arms around him, forcing him to lie down beside her. Her fingers worried over his head and back as she strained to listen to the sounds beyond the door. "Where are they? *Why* are they here?"

She hurried into her clothing and poured cereal into Omen's dish. "You're going to have to wait to pee, fella. I've got to investigate first. If there're people nearby . . ." She tried not to think about what might happen if their hiding place was discovered. "Be good, and *don't howl.* I'll be back soon."

As Billie scrambled up the apple tree, the bulldozer sounds grew louder. Across the road! Near the creek!

She dashed across the clearing, through the patch of forest that bordered the field. The grinding of machinery teeth and the crunching of trees trampled by huge chain-covered tires screamed over the wind-and-bird songs Billie had come to expect with each new day. Billie scanned the poplar cluster where she and Omen had spent their first night together, but the now-thick-leaved branches allowed only glimpses of the asphalt road. She drew in a deep breath and sprinted to the shelter. The whirring and rumbling echoed in her ears.

In the dense forest surrounding the creek, a huge pine tree crashed down, flattening smaller trees as it fell in slow motion toward the earth. A mustard-colored machine roared through the opening. Not a bulldozer at all, but some kind of small, powerful, tree-cutting machine. Its silver clamp-teeth bit into each tree, and it moaned as it swung out its blade arm, slashing the trunk straight through. It twisted about in a slow, menacing dance, spit out the tree, and rumbled toward another.

The opening across the road grew larger. In less than fifteen minutes, Billie could see clear to the hill which sloped down to the creek. A blue van pulled onto the shoulder of the road, and dread crept along Billie's arms as she read the printing on the side. K & D CONTRACTORS.

The engine shut off, and two men jumped from the van. One man pointed here and there while the other unrolled a big sheet of paper. They shouted to one another, but Billie couldn't hear the words over the roaring of the machine.

The sun moved higher into the sky, bright and warm, but as Billie ran to the underground room, cold, dark clouds gathered in her heart. Those people were going to build something right beside her creek! How would she and Omen get water—or fish or roots or—

Omen began to howl as soon as Billie reached the foundation. She had to squeeze into the room to keep Omen from shooting out the door.

"Trouble!" she said. "*Big* trouble, fella." She rummaged through her gear until she found the rope she was searching for. Omen whined and paced like a caged cougar. "I know," she said. "But you're going to have to let me go with you." She looped the rope around his neck. Immediately, Omen fell onto his side, digging at the rope with his hind legs.

Billie crouched in front of him, scratching under his chin. "Omen, this is serious, so listen to me." She tilted his head until their eyes met. "Those machines could run over you without even knowing it. You'd be coyote burger for the crows . . ." She snapped her fingers. ". . . that quick."

Omen's gaze stayed fixed on Billie's eyes.

"For now, we're going to leave our room and do our bathroom thing. But we can't go wandering around until after the tree-cutter and those contractor guys leave." She wrapped her end of the rope around her hand twice, then led Omen up the apple tree. "Looks like we're both going to have to become nocturnal."

Omen sniffed, then jerked his body toward the creek. As he stretched out his neck and jutted his head forward, Billie snapped her fingers against his nose. "No," she whispered. "You can't howl, no matter how crazy those sounds make you."

Omen lowered his head and let Billie pull him in the opposite direction. He remained quiet all through the long day, waiting, like Billie, for the sounds of bullfrogs to replace the roar of the awful machine across the road.

That night, with the light of the flashlight swinging in the room, she wondered what would be built across the road, and how long it would take to build it. How much longer before her secret room would be discovered?

Thursday, June 18. I may as well smash the music box—just like the machine is smashing the trees across the road. Omen'll die if I have to keep him on a leash his whole life, and the secret room is nothing without Omen.

He wouldn't go with me to the creek tonight. He took one whiff of the air near the parked machines, and high-tailed it across the road, whining like he'd been spooked by a ghost. His ears pricked up when the coyotes started singing, and he left.

I caught a good-sized trout for dinner, but Omen didn't come home to help me eat it. He'd better get back soon, or I'm going to go to sleep without him.

SEVENTEEN

Billie awoke late. "Eight-thirty!" she exclaimed as she scrambled from her covers. "Omen, you lazy pup," she muttered. "Why didn't you—"

Omen wasn't asleep beside her bed, or sniffing at the food on the shelves above. He wasn't pawing through her pile of painted rocks in the corner, either. Had Billie slept so soundly she hadn't heard him come back last night?

She shoved open the slatted door, hoping Omen was curled outside it. But Omen wasn't anywhere in the basement.

Machine sounds and cut-tree smells blew across the air above her. The K & D Contractors were back! How much more cutting were they going to do? Would they move across the highway, next, to Billie's fields and woods? She'd have to find out, but first, she had to find Omen.

She started for the woods, hoping he hadn't gone to the flute lady's garden. "O-men," she called, walking briskly, turning her head frequently so the wind would send her voice around the trees. Soon, he answered, but his howl was weak, muffled, as if someone had his hand over Omen's mouth.

Billie made a megaphone with her hands. *"Ar-r-r-ooo!"* she yipped, then waited for Omen's reply to lead her to him.

"Oh, Omen!" she cried, kicking blackberry branches out of her way. "I'm so sorry, fella." Thorns ripped at her hands as she worked to free him from the tangled rope. She'd forgotten the leash was still tied to his neck when he got spooked by the machines last night. "I'm so, so sorry." She tried to cradle him in her arms, but as soon as she slipped the rope off his neck, he dashed away. Billie followed at a dead run, not stopping until he led her into the secret room.

"No more rope, I promise," she told him, pouring cereal and milk and the last three strawberries into his bowl.

He slept all day, not even stirring when Billie washed up, put on clean jeans, and combed her hair. She left quietly in the afternoon.

As she weaved through the woods behind the foundation, she tried to judge how far to go before turning toward the highway. She didn't want to come out on the road too close to the place where the tree-chopping was happening. She thought about Omen, noosed in the blackberry thicket for how long? She could feel a tug at her own throat; even without a rope, the K & D Contractors were trapping her, too.

She left the woods and moved to the highway. She could hear the chain saws and machines up ahead, but she couldn't see the cleared place yet. She walked toward the sounds, planning what she'd say to the workers.

She crossed the road and waited in front of the blue van, watching huge green bulldozers scraping away violets and arbutus along with broken twigs and dark earth. She was glad she had found a way to make purple and pink nature-paint; at least the flowers on her pebbles were safe.

A man came around the back of the van, laughing. "Well, well, well, Sandra! Nothin' like a construction site to draw kids away from their T.V.s," he said.

Billie swallowed hard and shoved her hands into her pockets. She grinned at the man and shrugged.

"Children? Around here?" It was a woman's voice. Billie pressed her lips tight together to keep the gasp in her throat from escaping out loud.

Close up, the flute lady was taller than she looked bent over in the garden or playing songs on the porch. And rounder. Long strands of silver and black hair fluttered free from her loose ponytail. She flicked at them with the back of her hand. Now the owner of the garden had a voice; a name. It would be harder to steal spinach and berries after looking into the gardener's eyes.

"Hi, there!" she said, smiling from behind gold-wire glasses. "I didn't know there were any kids within miles of here." Her brow wrinkled slightly as she looked at Billie. It felt as if the lady were reading something in Billie's eyes. "Where do you live?"

Billie's gaze flitted back down the road. "I'm, uh . . . visiting . . . u-m-m . . . camping . . ." She stumbled over the words. The lady would know if there were campgrounds nearby, but Billie didn't.

"Camping, huh?" the contractor said. "Well, you tell your folks if they like it around here, I'll have the land cleared and divided into lots real soon." He turned to the flute lady and grinned; more of a smirk than a smile. "The creek lots will go fast."

The lady's eyes darkened to navy. "No one who enjoys camping will want these lots, Ken. Not after you've stripped all the trees away and chased off the wildlife!" Her arms and hands batted the air as she talked. "Nature should be preserved—and shared!" Her baggy flowered shorts flapped against her thighs as she stomped off.

"Ah! Everyone's a conservationist these days!" the man said, thrusting his arm in the direction of the lady's back. "Sandra's had this space to herself for too long. Thinks she owns it all, I guess." He chuckled.

I wish she did, Billie thought. "So how many houses are you going to build?" she asked, her voice attempting friendly curiosity. "When will you start?"

"First I divide the land," he said. "Probably eight good-sized lots." He looked up the road. The flute lady—Sandra—was no longer in sight. "Then I wait for folks to buy the lots. Building could start in a month or so, if business is good and the weather holds out."

Billie looked at her watch. "Well, I gotta go. Good luck with your business," she said. But all the way back along her camouflaged route to the secret room, Billie prayed for rain.

Omen was still sleeping when she returned, but he stretched and shook himself as she picked through her rocks, searching for the ones with the violet and arbutus blossoms. She set them on the shelf above her bed, then took a piece of birch bark from the highest shelf and began to scratch at it with a sharpened twig.

"Trees everywhere . . . the old pine branch hanging out over the creek where we lost our first fish . . ." she said as she etched the lines in the bark and the picture took shape. "That Ken guy can rip up the creek place, but he can't rip out the pictures in my head." And there's no Roger to tear up these pictures, she thought.

Along with the deepening dusk came the first wild yips from the distant forest. Billie washed the dishes and tamped down the fire to the sounds of Omen whimpering inside the closed room. Maybe the far-away coyotes were Omen's brothers and sisters; maybe Omen was searching for them when he got tangled in the blackberries. Maybe . . . maybe one day he'd *find* them. *Maybe it was time to let him try.* The thought stuck in Billie's throat like a fishbone as she watched Omen run into the night forest.

Her fingers worried the painted stone in her pocket during her entire hike to the big rocks. Probably the flute lady knew about the violets torn from the ground; maybe she'd like something to remember them by.

The flute lady—Sandra. "A snooty name," Ma

would have said. But the lady's eyes had been kind when she first greeted Billie, and they'd looked more pained than angry when she talked to the contractor about spoiling the land. Was Billie spoiling Sandra's land by taking from the garden, or was she simply sharing nature, like Sandra said people should do?

As usual, she was playing her flute in the shadows, the *creak-creaking* of the swing chains filling in the spaces between the notes. Billie got comfortable against the rocks, enjoying the private concert and the star-speckled sky. But when the music stopped, the lady called out, like before, "Is anyone out there?"

Billie clamped her hand over her mouth when Sandra got a reply.

"Whoo-whoo-whoot!"

Sandra laughed. *"Who-hoot,* yourself!" she said. "Where are you?" She craned her neck out over the railing.

"Whoo-whoot!"

"Indeed, it's a fine night, old wise one," she said.

After the screen door slammed, Billie stood cautiously. The porch swing was still swaying. Billie waited for the kitchen light to go out, for the upstairs light to brighten one of the second floor windows. Then she could get more berries. Just a few. She'd leave plenty for Sandra. Perhaps the peas were ripe, too.

Suddenly, the porch flooded with light from a bulb in the center. Billie ducked back behind the rocks. The door squeaked several times, as if someone were going in and out quietly, but quickly. She pressed her nose against the tallest boulder, rising slowly, until she could see what Sandra was doing and still stay hidden.

Sandra was standing directly under the porch light, leaning over a small table. Her fingers kneaded a large doughy brown lump as she stared into one of the apple trees. The owl was perched nearly at the top. It looked like he'd unscrew his head completely off as he turned it from side to side, and his eyes glowed when they caught the moonlight. Sandra continued talking to the owl as she worked the dark dough.

Clay! Billie realized. The garden lady—the flute lady—made the lawn sculptures herself! Sandra was a *real* artist.

The owl remained perched in the tree for nearly a half hour before it flew off, *who-whooing* farewells to Sandra. Sandra dipped a large cloth into a bucket and draped it over the clay lump. The towel was still dripping on the porch when she finally went inside and shut off the kitchen light.

Billie worked the garden rapidly. After she zipped the backpack, she pulled the painted stone from her pocket and set it under a large strawberry leaf. "It's not much," she whispered toward the house. "But it's all I've got to share right now."

The rain started before Billie reached the secret room, a light drizzle that worked itself into a driving downpour which continued through the night. Billie listened to the rain *thud-thudding* onto the ground above her, like thousands of wooden spoons beating upon hide-covered drums. Twice she opened the slatted door, yelling for Omen, but the crashing thunderbolts streaking through the darkness kept her calls trapped in the foundation.

In the morning, the rain still pounded overhead and pelted into puddles collecting in the basement. Billie soaked up the water seeping under the door with some dirty clothes, and waited for Omen to come home. There was no rope keeping him from getting back this time.

The strawberries and peas weren't nearly as tasty without Omen to share them, but she had to eat something. Her stomach was already squirmy enough without adding beetles to it.

As the hands of her watch moved slowly past afternoon, Billie took out her sketch pad. Sitting cross-legged on the rocker, she closed her eyes and pictured Omen asleep on the T-shirt near her bunk. She kept her eyes shut until she could imagine his sleep-sounds, then her fingers gripped the pencil and she began to draw. Night slipped over the land like a baggy shirt. Still, Billie drew, filling page after page of sketch paper with pictures of Omen.

EIGHTEEN

Wednesday, June 23. *The rain didn't keep Ken-the-contractor from his work too long. The day after the storm, the machines were back, bullying more trees and shoving uprooted ferns into giant dirt hills. I stay in this room most of the day, hearing Omen pawing and whining at the door, but it's never him; only wind-blown twigs and droning engines. And my hopes. I haven't seen Omen in four days.*

The contractors leave later and later each day. Last night it was after eight before I could call for Omen and fill my water jars and cook dinner. My pile of bark etchings is nearly as big as my pile of painted rocks now.

The garden lady—Sandra—found my painted stone! I went back to the rocks when the rain stopped on Monday. The early morning sun threw yellow stripes on the white porch boards while Sandra moved the clay under her hands. It was like magic the way she pinched and poked and ran flat wooden tools over the lump until it turned into the exact shape of the owl in the apple tree. Like magic, truly—but it took a long time. My legs were cramped when I came back to wait for Omen.

In the garden that night, I searched under the strawberry leaf for my painted stone. It was gone, but a tiny sculpture of a ladybug climbing a maple leaf was in its place! I stayed up late Monday night, copying one of my Omen pictures onto a piece of birch bark. Maybe if Sandra likes it, she'll make a coyote statue for her yard.

Since Omen's been gone, I've been having dreams about Roger. Sometimes Ma is in the dream, and Ma and Roger are laughing and dancing to the music box song and they don't know I'm in the dream with them. In other dreams, Ma is gone, and Roger is making tree-shaped pancakes for breakfast while a gray kitten purrs at my feet.

When people start building homes across the road, there won't be any safe time for building fires. And no way to get water. I can't stay here much longer. Maybe Omen already knows that.

Sometimes I sit here at night, thinking about Omen hunting with the wild coyotes. I imagine him grinning as they share a rabbit dinner. His smile is catching, and I smile, too. But only until I have to get into my bunk without Omen snoring beneath me. Before my dreaming starts, I tell myself that Omen wouldn't be happy without me. I tell myself that his Someplace and mine are the same. And if I think hard enough, sometimes I dream about a green field and an underground room where Omen and I grow up together.

Good stuff happens only in dreams, and then, not always.

NINETEEN

July and Omen arrived together, panting hot air through the door slats. As Billie lay on top of her sleeping bag, the thick, trapped cellar air kept her dreamy long after she'd awakened. Whimpering sounds seemed to echo from her sleep, but the scraping noise against the door was wide-awake insistent. Omen!

She nearly knocked him over when she flung the door open. She dropped to her knees and smothered him in hugs. "You had me scared half out of my wits," she said, wiping her cheeks against his fur. He sniffed his way into the room, his nose checking out every corner, every shelf, the rungs of the rocker.

"Yeah, you're home, fella," Billie said, tearing jerky into his bowl. When he'd lapped up every piece, he curled on his T-shirt bed.

Billie scratched under his chin and stroked the soft fur along his muzzle. The fur on his back wasn't as soft as she'd remembered; he was growing out of his baby coat. "Maybe you shouldn't have come back," she whispered to him. He lifted his head and peered at her. "Oh, don't get me wrong, buddy. I'm glad you wanted to see me. And if we could find a place without people, maybe we could stay together forever." Omen rested his head on his paws, but he kept watching her while she spoke, as if he knew Billie was painting a dream that wouldn't take.

She leaned closer, staring back at him. "What did you find out there, Omen? Did you find things I can't give you?" She shivered in the muggy room, then turned away from Omen as his eyes closed. "If *I* looked beyond our secret room, what would I find?"

While Omen slept, Billie sketched. And thought. Omen had been away for two weeks, but he had been fine on his own. He'd been brave, going into the woods, probably heading straight toward the songs of the wild coyotes. She closed the sketch book and put it near her duffle. This was Omen's Someplace; Billie wished it could be hers, too.

Quietly she sorted through her birch bark etchings until she found the one she'd made for Sandra. She mixed dandelion blossoms and water into a paste and colored in the eyes. She smiled.

Like gold marbles. Omen's eyes. She laid the picture on a shelf to dry, then turned her eyes to Omen. Biting her lip, she folded her arms tight across her chest, like a shield, and waited for Omen to wake.

The sounds at the building site were gone by seven thirty, but Billie ignored Omen's pacing in front of the door. She ignored the hungry rumblings in her stomach, and talked to Omen about the adventures they'd shared.

"Remember them, Omen," she whispered when her watch told her that the sky was dark.

Omen pranced around Billie's legs, prodding her hand with his nose.

"I'm not going with you tonight," she told him, drawing her hand away from him. "Not tonight—not ever again."

Hot tears rushed down her cheeks. She wrapped her arms over his back and clasped her hands under his belly. "I love you." She kissed his head. "I can't touch you anymore . . ." Sobs choked her. "Can't—leave—my scent—on your fur." She rubbed her face frantically on the back of his neck until she feared her tears would cling to him forever. She stood and opened the door, and forced her hands behind her back in fists.

"Now git! Go find your brothers and sisters!"

He dashed up the apple tree ramp, then stopped and turned his head. His gold marble eyes glistened in the moonlight as they stared down at Billie. His gaze moved back and forth between the dark woods and the place where Billie stood in the basement.

"Go *on*," Billie shouted. ". . . and *don't come back*!" Her nails dug into her palms.

Omen lowered his head and took a step toward the apple tree ramp. His ears pricked up at a sound Billie couldn't hear, and he turned and ran into the blackness.

"I love you, Omen," Billie whispered up after him.

Inside, she grabbed the shirt from Omen's spot beside her bunk, twisting it into knots. She settled into the rocker and set it in motion, cradling the shirt which had been Omen's bandage and his bed just as she'd held Omen that first night in the secret room. She rocked until her eyes were dry.

She took her time smoothing the wrinkles from the shirt, folding it carefully around the music box before she put them on the top shelf.

As she made her way to the rocks, she listened to the coyote songs. Perhaps Omen's voice was part of the chorus. Nearing the garden, Sandra's flute-playing mingled with the wild singing, then became distinct and separate. Billie tucked herself into the rocks and let the music soothe her invisible bruises.

Long after the last haunting note filtered down into Billie's den and the red door clicked shut, Billie remained against the rocks, thinking. Time was running out, and she had nowhere to go. She was farther now from Someplace than she'd ever been. She'd collect her things and leave the secret room tomorrow, and wait for another dream to find her along the way.

She clutched the birch bark tightly as she stepped around the rocks and walked among the clay creatures. Billie hoped the etching would be thanks enough for the free food and the nighttime concerts Sandra had unknowingly provided.

Keeping her eyes on the upstairs windows, she made her way through the grove of apple trees. Her foot was already on the bottom porch step when the kitchen light came on! She tossed the etching onto the porch and charged back through the orchard. Stumbling around the clutter of sculptures, she tried to picture where the small ones were. She leaped over the rabbit and the squirrel, but she hadn't known about the frogs and toads clustered together, low to the ground, near the deer. Her toe caught, sending her sprawling over them. Instantly, pain wrapped around her knee.

"Who's there?" Sandra called.

Sandra tromped down the steps, moving closer and closer. But Billie couldn't stand up. She was done running.

Sandra's footsteps quickened. With the whisper of her feet in the grass came the sound of parchment brushing against her clothing.

"Who's my mystery artist?" Sandra asked.

Billie made her body go limp as Sandra reached her. There was a soft groan, and the crackle of creaking joints as Sandra knelt and touched Billie's shoulder. Gently, she rolled Billie over.

"Oh, dear," she said, brushing tangled hair off Billie's face. "You're just—a child. Surely *you* aren't the artist—" She turned the etching toward Billie, then laid it carefully in the grass, her eyes full of questions. "The girl on the road a few weeks back!"

Billie sighed. Far in the distance, the coyotes yipped. She wished she could shout out, "*Ar-r-r-ooo*" and call them to her—call them to take her with them. But only Omen would understand, if he heard. Was he with the coyotes now, telling them his own story, hoping they would under-stand?

Above her, stars glittered like a billion silvery pearls stitched into an indigo blanket. *Glittering!* More shimmer and sparkle than Billie had seen during her entire journey.

"I am the artist," Billie said. "And I am your garden thief, too."

Sandra smiled. "It's said a picture is worth a thousand words..." She helped Billie into a sitting position, supporting Billie's back with her strong, clay-shaping hands. "...but in this case..." She grinned again. "In this case, I think we'll need an ample supply of words to fill in the spaces." She laced her arm under Billie's armpits and helped her up. "But first things first. Let's go inside and see what those foolish frogs have done to you!"

TWENTY

While she waited for her torn ligaments
to heal, Billie had listened for coyote sounds to
come through the open window in the bedroom
next to Sandra's. She liked to think that Omen
was part of the family of voices singing so freely in
the night. As the days went by, and she and
Sandra came to know one another, she began to
hope that the social workers would let her stay
with the gentle garden lady.

When Sandra first suggested that Billie stay
with her—forever—Billie was suspicious. Why
would a lady who had lived alone all her life suddenly want to take in some half-grown stray kid?
Maybe Sandra wanted someone to help with the
yard work and the housecleaning, for free. Billie
had read about people like that. She had to know
the real truth, to keep from building another
empty dream.

She waited until Sandra was busy re-wrapping
the bandage on her leg.

"Why do you want me to stay here with you?" she asked.

Sandra glanced up briefly, then turned back to Billie's bandages.

"I mean, my ma said kids are nothin' but trouble. Why would you want to bring trouble into your nice, quiet life?"

Sandra finished the wrapping and patted Billie's leg lightly. "Yes, some people feel that way." Her mouth was tight as she stared out the window. "I'm forty-seven years old. I thought I'd never get a chance to have a child in my life. And then you happened into my garden, and—" She shrugged and threw her hands out to the side. "I figured I'd trust the process. If it was meant to be, well . . ." She fluffed up Billie's pillow and handed her a magazine. "We'll see, won't we?"

Billie thought about Sandra's words. "Trust the process," she'd said. Maybe Billie would try that. If this was her Someplace, she'd sing when Sandra played her flute, and together they'd send their music over the treetops to the coyotes.

"We have to be patient," Sandra told Billie. "It takes time to check everything out."

"Don't they trust me?" Billie had asked. "Don't they believe that there isn't any family to take me in—that Roger doesn't want a kid in his life?"

"It's just the system, sweetheart," she said, moving toward the door. "And it's good for them to check everything out. It protects people. In the end, it'll be best for you and me, you'll see."

When Billie no longer needed crutches, she crept from the bed every night to look out at the moon-swept yard—and wait for the breezes to blow coyote concerts to her ears.

Sandra suggested making a coyote sculpture the day she was given temporary custody of Billie.

"Temporary!" Billie had shouted. "My whole life has been one *temporary* after another!"

"Legal guardianship can't be hurried, Billie." Sandra had smiled then. "Every day we spend together is permanent for twenty-four hours!" She led Billie to the porch. "The pleasures in the todays give me faith to look forward to the tomorrows."

She began working her hands over a huge mass of wet clay. "Come," she said, taking Billie's hands in her clay-covered ones. "There's important work to be done while we wait." She dipped Billie's hands in the warm, reddish-brown water, then moved her hands on top of Billie's, pressing them lightly into the soft clay.

"What are you making?" Billie asked.

"I'm not making anything," Sandra said,

"—*we* are making something!" She laughed. "I'd like to make a coyote; what would you like to make?"

Billie massaged the clay, feeling for Omen's muscles under her fingers. She closed her eyes and moved her hands across the lump of moist earth, imagining his head, trying to remember how far along his back her hands traveled to reach his tail. She opened her eyes. "Yes," she said. "A coyote."

They worked on the sculpture for many days before it was ready to be fired in Sandra's kiln. "When it's time for painting," Sandra said, "I think you should do his eyes. I'd never be able to capture them as you knew them."

They stood back to admire their work. It was so real-looking it could have been Omen. Billie had to resist the urge to reach out and wait for his breath to pant against her hand.

"No matter what happens," Sandra said, "the sculpture is yours."

Before Billie knew it, her arms were around Sandra's waist, and Sandra's soft middle was pillowing her head. Billie didn't resist when Sandra hugged back.

A week before school started, Sandra dragged the heavy sculpture on a dollie and slid it to the ground just beyond the garden fence. "In honor of Omen, who guided you here," Sandra said. "Maybe he'll come by some night for a visit."

That had been a month ago, but as far as Billie knew, Omen had not yet visited the clay coyote. Now, as Billie crossed the highway and stopped at the place where she'd heard Omen whimpering nearly seven months earlier, the air was October-crisp. Billie and Sandra were still waiting for the official decision, for the legal papers that would declare them a permanent family. But the sculpture they had created was baked-hard and glazed to last forever already. Billie's memories were indestructible, too.

Behind her, Sandra's jeep idled, keeping Sandra warm while Billie returned to the secret room for the first time since the accident near the garden. Billie shined Sandra's flashlight through the trees, searching for the exact spot where Omen had been curled in the blood-stained snow. A chilly wind blew memories of drain pipes and abandoned sheds against Billie's face. Tonight she'd sleep under Ma's quilt in a soft bed, with warm flute lullabies climbing the stairs to the bedroom. Where did Omen sleep now?

She knew the way to the old foundation by heart; there was no need to depend on the flashlight yet. Light flurries flecked in the moonlit air as she shinnied down the apple tree ramp and kicked through dried leaves which had collected in her absence.

Her flashlight, left behind when Sandra retrieved her things and brought them back to the house, still hung from the ceiling string. She clicked the button and soft light began to sway around the room. The old chair creaked familiar music as she rocked, and images of Omen echoed off the walls.

By next summer, Omen would be grown up, the same size as the statue. Billie might be able to push back the blue bedroom curtains and imagine Omen there, standing guard over the vegetables, as attentive as he'd been while he was guarding her.

The old flashlight wasn't the only thing left behind in the secret room. On the highest shelf, the T-shirt looked like nothing more than a wadded-up rag. Billie brushed away the cobwebs and unwrapped the plastic music box.

She carried the music box up the ramp and sat near the blackberry thicket, its branches now bare and brittle and tangled. Billie turned toward the woods. *"Ar-r-r-ooo!"* she shouted into the darkness.

The only sound was the wind blowing through the pines.

"*Ar-r-r-ooo! Ar-r-r-ooo!*"

She held the music box on her lap and waited. She'd sit there the whole night if she had to. "*Ar-r-r-ooo, ar-r-r-ooo.*"

Something scampered through the brush, and Billie's heart leapt. But the sound was of something small, not Omen's ground-vibrating thrashing. She fastened the storm flap across her chin and blew hot breath into her hands. And she waited.

"*Ar-r-r-ooo, ar-r-r-ooo,*" she called, over and over and over, until her throat burned and her hands were stiff from cupping them around her mouth. Tucking the music box inside her coat, she turned back toward the highway.

She stopped in the middle of the field. The wind had calmed. In the distance, far beyond the woods where Omen had done his best hunting, came the sound: a single coyote. "*Ar-r-r-ooo-oooo!*"

Hurriedly, Billie wound the music box, holding the dancers at the top, just as Ma had done last Christmas morning. The howling grew louder and louder as more coyotes joined the soloist in the plaintive, wild song.

When the voices began to fade, Billie released her hold on the dancers, and the music began. *There's a magical someplace with songs to sing . . .*

The couple twirled in an endless circle, dancing under the moon to the tinny tune. Billie danced too, until the music box wound down, and it was time to go home.

BIBLIOGRAPHY

BEHME, ROBERT L. *SHASTA & ROGUE.* NEW YORK: SIMON AND SCHUSTER, 1974.

BRONSON, WIFRID S. *COYOTES.* SAN DIEGO, CALIFORNIA: HARCOURT, BRACE AND COMPANY, INC., 1946.

DEBAUCHE, JACKIE. DIRECTOR OF REHABILITATION, NORTHWOODS WILDLIFE CENTER, MINOCQUA, WISCONSIN. PERSONAL AND TELEPHONE INTERVIEWS.

DOBIE, J. FRANK. *THE VOICE OF THE COYOTE.* PHILADELPHIA, PENNSYLVANIA: CURTIS PUBLISHING COMPANY, 1949.

JONES, J. KNOX AND ELMER C. BIRNEY. *HANDBOOK OF MAMMALS OF THE NORTH CENTRAL STATES.* MINNEAPOLIS, MINNESOTA: UNIVERSITY OF MINNESOTA PRESS, 1988.

RUE, LEONARD LEE III. *FURBEARING ANIMALS OF NORTH AMERICA.* NEW YORK: CROWN PUBLISHERS, 1981.